Blood in the Water

Gillian Galbraith

Polygon

First published in 2007 by Crescent Crime
an imprint of Mercat Press
and reprinted in 2007

This edition published in 2008 by Polygon
an imprint of
Birlinn Limited
West Newington House
10 Newington Road
Edinburgh
EH9 1QS

www.polygonbooks.co.uk

ISBN-13: 978 1 84697 074 0
eBook ISBN: 978 0 85790 013 5

Reprinted in 2012

Set in Italian Garamond BT at Mercat Press

Printed and bound in Great Britain by
Clays Ltd, St Ives plc

Blood in the Water

Gillian Galbraith

grew up near Haddington in Scotland. For several years she practised as an Advocate specialising in medical negligence and agricultural law cases. She was the Legal Correspondent for the *Scottish Farmer* and has written law reports for *The Times. Blood in the Water*, her first book, was published in 2007. A second Alice Rice mystery, *Where the Shadow Falls* (2008), was followed by three others, *Dying of the Light* (2009), *No Sorrow to Die* (2010) and *The Road to Hell* (2012). She lives deep in the country near Kinross with her husband and child, cats, dogs, hens and bees.

Other titles in the Alice Rice series:

Where the Shadow Falls
Dying of the Light
No Sorrow to Die
The Road to Hell

Acknowledgements

With grateful thanks for all their help to: David Bowen, Douglas Edington, Lesmoir Edington, Diana Griffiths, Jinty Kerr, Dr Elizabeth Lim, Aidan O'Neill and Alisdair White. Any errors in the text are my own.

Dedication

To Ma, with all my love

I

Thursday 1st December

'Look, you can see it on the screen. That's the baby... there. It's now about, say, two inches from crown to rump and weighs, maybe, a quarter of an ounce... you can see the little heart beating... and everything that should be there seems to be there...'

Dr Clarke slid the transducer over her patient's pregnant belly, keeping a careful eye at all times on the black and white image on the ultrasound screen. Mrs Greig smiled and grasped her husband's hand more tightly. He craned over her towards the screen, attempting to make out, amongst all the shades of grey, any recognisable human form.

'Can you tell the sex yet?' he asked.

'No. The sex organs only begin to differentiate in the third month, and even then assessing gender can be difficult. We'll do a more detailed scan later on in the pregnancy and we should get a better idea at that stage. Otherwise, if you are having amniocentesis the fluid can be checked and a more certain result given. What are you hoping for?'

'A girl,' Mr Greig said firmly.

'A healthy child, girl or boy,' his wife corrected.

'Well, I'll see you in about six weeks time when we'll take blood for the AFP estimation. In the meanwhile, you'll be under the care of your GP, but don't hesitate to contact the hospital if you have any problems.'

As Dr Clarke left the ultrasound room her patient was getting dressed. The white-coated consultant walked slowly towards her office, wondering why she felt tired so early in the day. She glanced at her watch registering that she had twenty minutes before she was scheduled to start her twelve o'clock Monday appointment in the High Risk Maternity Clinic. Sufficient time for a cup of coffee and a skim of the newspaper. The office that had been allocated to her for the morning was small and uncomfortable. One entire wall was occupied by textbooks and periodicals, and a desk-top computer with all the paraphernalia associated with it seemed to have taken over the rest of the room. The sole window was obscured by a large leafy pot plant, a legacy from the previous occupant, which despite getting the lion's share of any available light was in the process of dying untidily. The much reviled architecture of the new Royal Infirmary at Little France came out well in comparison with this, at least, and her own bolt-hole in the new hospital now seemed palatial in comparison to these dingy quarters. Clearing a stack of charts from the seat of the only chair available, she sat down and took a sip of her black brew.

Elizabeth Clarke was a tall woman, elegant in an understated way, with greying brown hair and pale blue eyes which communicated little emotion and surveyed the world with a distant, unblinking gaze. Her permanent expression of slight disdain and regal carriage gave her a patrician air, powerful enough to ward off all but the most confident. She wore almost no make-up, the slightest brush of mascara, but had begun to wonder whether she could still afford so little assistance with her appearance. As she began to daydream her mind drifted, once more, to her life and the absence of any man in it. They only complicate things, she thought, better no man than the wrong one, experience had taught her that much. But no sooner had she reassured herself than the voice of doubt whispered in her ear that she was too critical, unnaturally choosy, incapable of looking at any man other than as a potential spouse, and that she must change, learn to live in the moment and let things take their natural course, stop analysing every relationship to death and expecting perfection. She should settle for an ordinary, flawed mortal like everyone else. Her meditation was ended by the harsh tones of her beeper signalling the arrival of her first patient in the High Risk Clinic. Downing the dregs of her coffee, she rose to her feet and began to pick up the pile of medical records on her desk.

Eleanor Hutton was well-known to Dr Clarke. A patient who, more often than not, was the author of her many misfortunes and considered all advice given to her as optional. This was her fifth pregnancy, another 'mistake', and each new gestation had been more difficult to supervise than the last. The woman was a law unto herself. In between babies she turned up, erratically, at the Diabetes Clinic, usually when her condition was completely out of control. For a few weeks she would take note of whatever strictures had been directed at her, only to relapse into her careless ways until the next time. She was fat, jolly and untidy, invariably clad in tight clothes usually revealing, in unexpected places, rolls of white flesh. Dr Clarke, against her better judgement, liked her patient.

'But I ken whit I'm daein backwards, doctor...' Eleanor protested.

'Yes, Eleanor, but you must turn up for your appointments, all your appointments. You've missed the last three. We've no recent record of your weight, the baby's size, whether it has been moving as it should, the foetal heart rate. There's been no booking scan, you're unsure about your last menstrual period, we haven't been able to test your urine... Where do I begin?'

'Ehm... ma diabeetis is under control,' the patient volunteered, to placate her physician.

'Maybe. As you don't do half your blood-sugar tests I'm not convinced you'd know. I've told you before you are exposing your baby to a real risk. If this is another big one—and Debbie was over eleven pounds, wasn't she?—it might die in the womb. These big babies sometimes do, often shortly before they're due to be delivered. So we need to monitor their health, their size, particularly carefully… And you smoked all during your last pregnancy.' Dr Clarke was unable to suppress a sigh of exasperation.

'Ye'll see, doctor, I'll attend frae noo on. You jist tell me when tae turn up and I'll be there. I've gi'en up the fags this time, gi'ed them up as soon as I kent I wis expecting.' Eleanor smiled broadly, exposing denture-free gums, evidently considering, as usual, that her assurances of past and future compliance would be taken at face value.

'If you have difficulty getting to the hospital I can, if necessary, arrange for you to be picked up by an ambulance for your appointment,' Dr Clarke persisted.

'I'll be there doctor, dinnae worry yerself again.'

Dr Clarke left the clinic musing over the unfairness of human reproduction. Patients like Eleanor Hutton conceived as soon as blink, were careless of the health of their unborn children and yet usually carried to term. Others tried and tried, mangling their sex lives in the process, resorting to every quack device on the market only to conceive and then lose the child despite their meticulous care.

Collecting her coat and a battered leather case bulging with papers from her office, she left Lauriston Place and the old Royal Infirmary buildings and set off in the direction of South Bridge. When she got to Blackwells bookshop, she stopped to browse amongst the CDs in the music department and eat a hurried sandwich. On emerging onto the wet street, she congratulated herself on making only one purchase, Elgar's 'Sea Pictures' with Janet Baker. Temptation was usually succumbed to more fully; you could not have too many CDs. Crossing the road, she noticed, at a bus stop on the other side, Eleanor Hutton standing sheltering from the persistent drizzle. The pregnant woman was smoking a cigarette. The doctor was aware of a further temptation, the temptation to snatch the fag from the woman's mouth and stamp it out on the wet pavement in front of her. Instead, hoping to embarrass her patient into some minimum of care for her unborn child, she simply gave a nod of recognition, watching intently as Mrs Hutton, on meeting her eyes, surreptitiously dropped her cigarette to the ground and extinguished the lipstick-stained stub with the heel of her boot.

'It's ma last yin, doctor, ye ken hoo nervous I aye get in hospitals. Nae mair fi' noo oan.'

Dr Clarke nodded politely again, inwardly acknowledging the futility of any further discussion.

McDonald House, the building containing the Faculty of Advocates' consulting rooms, was recessed off the High Street down a small, ill-lit wynd. Its large, well-furnished waiting room was warm, plentifully stocked with glossy magazines and reminiscent of a slightly stuffy gentleman's club forced, unwillingly, into the twenty-first century. As Dr Clarke lowered herself thankfully into a red leather armchair, *CD World* in hand, Kate McLeod, her solicitor from the Scottish Health Service Central Legal Office, spotted her and came to sit next to her. The young woman's face and clothes were streaked with rain, and she hauled behind her a large shopping trolley, weighed down with blue cardboard files. Seeing the doctor's quizzical gaze on it, she volunteered that all her colleagues were supplied with the trolleys in order, they assumed, for their employers to avoid any liability for injuries caused by the carrying of the reams of paper needed for most consultations. Extracting one of the files from the trolley, she opened it and handed the doctor a two-page document, explaining that it had just been e-mailed to her by their opponents, and was a report from the pursuer's expert witness, Dr Manning.

While Elizabeth Clarke was reading the report, two men dressed in black jackets and waistcoats, with sponge-bag trousers and shiny shoes, approached her armchair. Looking up, she recognised Robert Philip QC and his Junior, Simon

Stewart. Both were known to her from previous court battles. The Silk was a fat man; his starched collar disappeared into the folds of his neck and two pendulous dewlaps overshadowed his tie. Yards of white shirt were visible in the gap between his waistcoat and his trousers, and a gold fob watch chain strained across his belly, emphasising its prosperous rotundity. His Junior was also corpulent, but looked less likely to melt on a hot day, some signs of muscle and bone still apparent.

After cursory greetings they went downstairs, the Silk leading the way to room fourteen, took their seats and laid out their papers on the large mahogany table that dominated the chamber. Once seated, Dr Clarke was irritated to find that she felt nervous. She was conscious that her heart was beating, thumping against her chest, and that the place had suddenly become uncomfortably warm and airless. It was so stupid, this fear. She had no reason to feel apprehensive, no cause for any anxiety. All that they wanted was her expert opinion, an opinion she was eminently qualified to provide. Breathing slowly in and out, she reminded herself, it's not me this time, it's not me that they're after.

Robert Philip quickly sketched out the case, reading when necessary from the Closed Record. It was a medical negligence action. A woman had gone into hospital for a sterilisation operation, involving the blocking of her fallopian tubes. The surgeon treating her had performed, before the sterilisation operation, a dilatation and curettage procedure. His patient had, allegedly, not consented to the additional procedure. Subsequently, she had developed septicaemia. She attributed the development of the septicaemia to the unauthorised 'D&C', and now wanted compensation from the NHS Trust responsible for the hospital.

Listening to the crisp, unemotional summary of events, Dr Clarke wondered whether the lawyers involved had any idea of the degree of concern that a suit, such as that being so coolly discussed, engendered in the doctors under attack. Whether they liked it or not, they would have to live with the allegation of negligence day after day, probably for up to six years or so, until they were found guilty or innocent of the charge against them. To exonerate themselves they would have to endure days in a witness box being harangued by an aggressive young Turk intent upon making his reputation by destroying theirs. Any hidden insecurities they felt in carrying out their difficult jobs were exacerbated by the litigation and would eat away at them. Even if the case against them was finally dismissed, their professional confidence was dented, the shadow of a stain on their record.

The afternoon passed slowly, with Dr Clarke explaining in detail precisely what was involved, in surgical terms, with a D&C procedure and a sterilisation operation using fallope rings. When asked, she drew, on paper thrust hurriedly before her, diagrams of the relevant anatomy, the uterus, cervix, fallopian tubes and ovaries, and Robert Philip quickly scrawled the names of the organs, or structures, onto her drawings. As she spoke, Junior Counsel took copious notes in his old fashioned blue jotter and, she observed with amusement, sketched caricatures of his Senior whenever she became remotely repetitious. Before long the atmosphere in the windowless room became heavy with the odour of warm work-clothing, and she was much relieved when Philip announced, at about six pm, that their meeting would have to end, as he had to pick up his child from kindergarten. Not for the first time she considered the fate of the offspring of the professional classes, in a nursery or some other care practically from birth onwards, their needs always secondary to their parents' ambition. Better not have a child at all, for the child's sake; there was no longer any question in her mind about that. It was a modern myth, this 'having it all' for women, about as achievable as a cache of fairy gold or a clutch of phoenix's eggs. Choices had to be made, and she had made hers.

The air outside was cold, a sharp refreshing cold after the foetid warmth of the consulting room. Deliberately exhaling the used air from her lungs, she breathed in deeply and, pulling up the collar of her dark blue coat, walked up the High Street towards the Castle, turning right to go down the Mound towards Princes Street. She felt a surge of childish delight on seeing the mass of white lights on the huge Christmas tree opposite the twin gothic towers of Playfair's New College, the brilliant strands swinging wildly in the wind that was beginning to rise. In ten minutes the Dean Bridge and her home at 1 Bankes Crescent came into view, partially obscured by the bare winter trees that flanked the north side of the Dean Gardens. She removed her gloves to unlock the impressive black front door that served the three flats and picked up her mail. Nothing more than the usual advertising circulars and a couple of dull looking brown envelopes. No Christmas cards yet.

Elizabeth Clarke had never subscribed to the view that drinking alone amounted to the taking of the first, few, faltering steps along the road to perdition. A maxim coined by some bibulous married man, never short of domestic company. Anyway, if it did, she was half-way to hell already and quite determined to reach journey's end. The long gin and tonic she poured herself would simply allow her taut mind to relax, enabling her to enjoy the Elgar more fully and dull the shrill, ever-present voice in her head which told her that she should be doing something, achieving something. She took the new disc from its box, put it into her CD player and switched the sound to the speakers in her bathroom.

The warm water enveloped her, caressed her aching limbs. She stretched out her arm lazily for her mobile phone, thinking that once she had spoken to her mother she would be free of all responsibilities, at least until after supper, when she would have to compile the medical report commissioned by those aggressive solicitors in Glasgow.

'Hello Ma, it's me. How's your back been?'

'It's much better, darling, it's really the pains down my legs that are more troublesome now, but they're beginning to lessen. I've been taking those anti-inflammatories you told me about. More importantly, how are you? How was work today?'

'Fine. I was at the old Royal Infirmary for a clinic, probably one of the last I'll ever have there, I expect, so I didn't have to take the car to Little France for a change. I'd almost forgotten what a pleasure it can be to walk to work. In the afternoon, I had to consult in a legal case in the High Street and I could go straight there from the hospital. Otherwise much as usual. I'm glad your back's better. I wondered whether you had any idea what you'd like for Christmas? I thought you might enjoy that new book on the Mitfords, and I could get you some fine soap too. What do you think?'

'I got the Mitford book from the library yesterday, but I'd love the soap. What about you, have you thought of anything? Is there any new disc you'd like?'

'Not at the moment. I'd like a surprise. I know it's more difficult but I'd prefer it if you can be bothered. By the way, I got excellent news today, I'm off on Christmas Day and Boxing Day so I'll be able to come home and spend a night. We might even manage a service at St. Mary's.'

'Wonderful! I was beginning to think that we were going to be out of luck this year. I'll order a turkey from Fenton Barns and we'll get a ham too. You'll be pleased to hear that Aunt Judith can't make it, she's…'

'Sorry Ma, I'm going to have to go. Someone's ringing the doorbell. I'll phone you back later tonight or sometime tomorrow evening.'

Dr Clarke put down the phone, dressed in haste and ran to the front door. Despite the delay her caller was still waiting for her.

2

Friday 2nd December

An icy wind blew on platform twelve of Waverley Station. A wind that cut like a cold blade through clothing, and which seemed to have travelled unimpeded from the steppes of Siberia. While her fellow-passengers huddled together in groups like cattle in a snowstorm, each gaining shelter from the other, Detective Sergeant Alice Rice paced up and down the length of the platform in a futile attempt to keep warm and make the train arrive sooner. She stopped her restless activity only to listen to the flat tones of the station announcer:

'The train from Glasgow due to arrive on platform twelve at nine am has been delayed and is now expected at nine-fifteen am.'

No more than a bland statement of fact. The bulletin tailed off without explanation or apology. While Alice was digesting this information and considering whether she could be bothered to put pen to paper to complain, a little man, smelling strongly of drink, sidled up to her. His clothes had 'charity shop' written all over them. Oversized black plastic shoes with pristine brown laces, ill-fitting sheepskin coat and fake cavalry twill trousers exposing nylon Argyll-patterned socks. One of the hopeless combinations of poverty, drink and middle age, to whom the capital could no longer offer a home. She became aware of the stench of warm lager fumes close to her face.

''Lo, hen,' he exhaled into her breathing zone.

She could have moved away, pretending to have heard nothing, but she chose instead to respond, thinking it would make the time pass more quickly.

'Hello,' she replied, smiling in a half-hearted fashion. Sensing a green light the drunk immediately launched into a practised monologue, something about Glasgow's virtues and Edinburgh's vices, meandering into the state of Scottish football and the Pope's nazi past. He seemed to require only an occasional nod from Alice to keep up his inane patter. Before he could start on a new topic, Alice became aware of a train drawing up on the platform. She smiled politely at the little man and, intending to detach herself from him, began to move along the train looking for a less-crowded carriage near the front. A journey of over fifty minutes in his company, in a badly ventilated space, would be beyond the call of charity, duty or anything else. She settled down at a table for four, occupied only by an austere-looking woman wearing blue-tinted spectacles. She looked up from her newspaper momentarily to see who was intruding into her space. As Alice unfastened her briefcase and took a copy of a statement from it she became aware of the familiar scent of stale lager. She glanced up to see the grinning face of her small companion as he edged himself towards the vacant seat by her side. He flopped down into it noisily, introducing an additional smell, the sweet, sickly smell of the unwashed.

''Lo, hen.'

This time the greeting was directed at the bespectacled lady passenger who, in an attempt to avoid engaging in conversation with anyone, seemed to have shrunk into herself. In response she smiled, with her mouth only, at the drunk, and then immediately lowered her eyes again. If she believed that the coolness of her response would stop any further unwelcome conversation she was wrong.

'Hen. Hen!' he persisted. 'This lady…'—he gestured expansively towards Alice—'…this lady's ma wife, Mary. We've been married about ten years now. Oh, we've had our ups and doons, what couple's no, but I've stuck by her through thick and thin and she's always…'—he gazed at Alice fondly—'been there for me…'

Alice was paralysed by surprise into inaction. As the urge to dissociate herself from the drunk, even to a stranger, grew, she heard him say:

'We've just been blessed with the one bairn. A wee boy. We cry him Jesus.'

'Excuse me,' Alice said to the woman opposite, 'before this journey I'd never met this man. He is not my husband. We have no child.'

The woman nodded her understanding and Alice found herself then smiling, weakly, at the little man. She wondered why on earth she was smiling at him. A desire to avoid hurting his feelings after this public rejection? No, more likely a concern to avoid any transition in him from affability to aggression. He was drunk and Scottish after all. Having successfully unnerved the two female passengers, the man closed his eyes and began, in what seemed to be seconds only, to snore loudly.

Glasgow Sheriff Court was packed with people: a strange assortment of sharp-suited lawyers, anxious-looking litigants, police, social workers and sullen-faced criminals. As Alice was trying to find out from the reception desk which court she was due to attend, she was tapped on the shoulder. Turning, she recognised Anna O'Neil, Deputy Procurator Fiscal, and an old friend from university.

'The trial's off…' Anna said. 'The accused pled guilty to a lesser charge. You won't be needed. The advocate depute's released all the witnesses.'

A broad grin spread across Alice's face. She could have shouted for joy, the relief at not having to appear in court was so immense. She had prepared herself for the ordeal, felt ready for it, but experienced not a tinge of regret that she would be deprived of the opportunity to voice the testimony she had been rehearsing in her head for the last few days.

Alice Rice had entered the police force, on the accelerated promotion scheme for graduates, in the belief that whatever else such a career could lack, it would, always, provide interest. A challenging job, not necessarily well paid but with endless variety and the chance to do something worthwhile. It had taken only a few months on the beat for her to realise that a great deal of the work was mundane, repetitious and thankless. Fortunately, she was an optimist, believing that as she progressed up the organisation the new horizons facing her would be stimulating and to some extent this had proved true.

But there was a cost attached. She hated the process of giving evidence as a witness. Each time she had to do it she dreaded the next more, and yet the task was central to the job. There was no way of avoiding it, and bad luck seemed to arrange matters so that she spent hours being cross-examined when her colleagues were in and out of the box having given little more than their names. No-one could have been more meticulous in their preparation for court, but for all the hard hours spent, she invariably was left feeling that the accused's lawyer, wily solicitor or new-born advocate, had got the better of her. How could she be so easily tripped up, when all she was doing was trying, to the best of her ability, to tell the truth?

And there was another insidious effect of the job that she was becoming increasingly aware of and disconcerted by. She no longer seemed to be at home anywhere, at ease, anywhere. Her gender, resolute middle-classness and graduate status all marked her off as alien within the force, and now even in the civilian world she often found herself adrift. Her friends from university, with one exception, had all gone into either the law, publishing or business. None of them had ever had a handful of their hair wrenched out by a distraught female shoplifter, or been spat at by an irate protester. They would never have to tell the parents of a small child that he'd been killed by a drunken driver on his way home from school. The points of contact between her world and that of her friends seemed to be growing fewer as time passed.

Also, and it was a big also, she was the only one to have remained unmarried, unpartnered and childless into her thirty-fifth year. Her single state was easily explained. It was not that she was unattractive, quite the reverse; she was positively good-looking, being tall, just over six feet, clear-skinned and with dark hair and hazel eyes. Men were attracted to her as wasps to jam on a late summer afternoon. The real problem, in her estimation at least, lay in her unashamed independence, which gave the impression of complete self-sufficiency. It was, in fact, a front created by her in childhood and which she had never since had the courage to discard.

No vegetation adorned the stern lines of the St Leonard's police station. Its dirty, yellow-ochre brick met the dull grey of the pavement seamlessly, and the only concession to the fad of landscaping community buildings had been the planting of a few rowan trees, now sickly and requiring the protection of metal grilles. Inside, the station was humming. News of a killing on the north side had just come in from the station at Gayfield Square and the chosen murder squad was assembling for its first briefing from Detective Chief Inspector Elaine Bell. Alice stuffed her bacon roll back into its brown paper bag while scanning the unoccupied seats for Alastair Watt's friendly face. Back row, third from the left. The team could have been much worse, she decided. She would have to work with him, DCs Irwin, Littlewood, McDonald and Sinclair, and the only fly in the ointment was the inclusion of Eric Manson, Detective Inspector Manson. She reached the vacant chair next to Alastair just as DCI Bell began her briefing.

'As you will all know by now, there has been a murder in Bankes Crescent, and officers from Gayfield Square are in attendance at present. The victim is a Dr Elizabeth Clarke, a medical consultant, aged about forty-one. She was found in her flat at No. 1 Bankes Crescent this morning round about nine am by her cleaning lady, a Mrs Ross, when she let herself in. We don't have much information so far, but it seems that she was killed by having her throat cut, probably some time about six to twelve hours ago. A little piece of lined paper with the word 'unreliable', written in green biro, was found at the victim's feet. Gayfield have already taken some statements, but I'd like Alice and Alastair to interview Dr Clarke's nearest neighbours. Get the usual stuff plus any information that you can about the victim. Eric can go to the Royal Infirmary, the new building, to speak to the doctor's colleagues at work. I've already spoken to a Dr Maxwell, from her department, and I'd suggest beginning with him. He worked beside the victim for years…'

DCI Bell looked pale, ivory white with blue-black rings bordering her eyes, unconcealable by any make-up. She was a workaholic, and her addiction, knowingly nurtured by her superiors, was destroying her health. The everyday business of the station overloaded her already frayed circuits, and the additional workload imposed by the killing would likely result in a burn-out of some kind. For the duration of the investigation she would become, like most of those involved, an occasional visitor to her own home and her husband provided scant sympathy, having long been disenchanted with 'the force' and its unreasonable demands. The woman he had married had yearned for a home and children and, in their absence as the years went by, had metamorphosed into an alien creature, more accustomed to giving orders than taking them.

The location of Dr Clarke's flat was obvious from the number of police vehicles parked outside the imposing stone building that began the crescent and abutted Eton Terrace. A young constable, still too thin for his uniform, was on duty logging movements in and out of the big black front door. The building was attached to its neighbour by a monumental screen wall with three blind arches, resembling three closed eyes. It overlooked the Dean Gardens, an area perfumed with the unlikely scent of beer from the Water of Leith that passed through it, having collected brewery effluent further upstream. Dressed in paper suit and bootees, Alice climbed the thickly carpeted stair that led to Elizabeth Clarke's flat. The outer hall was painted a deep oxblood red, and a number of small watercolours of naval ships decorated its walls. Noting that photographers and other scene-of-crime officers were busy in the drawing room, she took a detour into the doctor's study instead. It was dominated by a pair of large, shiny, black speakers. They were entirely out of keeping with the rest of the furniture in the room, all of which had been arranged to allow them pride of place. The floor was covered in neat piles of papers and copies of medical journals had been filed, by title, along the skirting-boards. A Georgian writing desk lay open with a set of original medical records on it, yellow post-it stickers protruding from some of the papers.

She moved to the victim's bedroom, on the upper floor, and found it almost monastic in its orderliness. The bedclothes had been turned back in expectation of the night to come, and on a bare table by the bed were three books, a novel by Lermontov and two textbooks: *Fetal Monitoring in Practice* and *Obstetrics by Ten Teachers*. The air was heavy with the scent of freesias: a huge vase of the yellow flowers had been placed on the windowsill and, as in the study, a pair of large black speakers was present. There was no other furniture in the room. A white panelled door led from it into an en suite bathroom, and all of the four walls within were composed of mirrors. Disconcertingly, on entering the bathroom, Alice found herself reflected from every angle, a few white hairs evident amongst the brown now. She wondered how anyone could endure, never mind enjoy, such unvarnished scrutiny every time they entered the place, far less undressed in it. The bath was still full, the water bluish with dissolved soap, and an opened copy of the *Spectator* lay discarded on the still wet bathmat. The room felt as if its occupant might return at any minute.

Alice left and went downstairs to the living room, which bustled with professionals intent on doing their jobs, the victim's body already having been removed. A huge area of pale carpet in front of a chintz-covered sofa, and the sofa itself, was suffused with dark blood. It had splattered onto the high ceiling, dripped onto the ornate cornice and one of the walls. Two large oil paintings, views of Edinburgh in the nineteenth century, had splashes on them as if Jackson Pollock had been let loose to improve them with a bucket of red paint. Aware that she was in the way of the fingerprint men, she moved into an ante-room and found every inch of wall space taken up by shelf after shelf of CDs. The size of the woman's collection rivalled her own, and a cursory inspection suggested their tastes were similar too. A huge metallic CD player stood in the centre of the small room, like a silver idol, and a series of switches were labelled, in cramped, irregular handwriting, 'bedroom', 'bathroom', 'study' and 'kitchen'. Elgar's 'Sea Pictures' was in the machine.

Alastair Watt entered the shrine, his large bulk suddenly making the space, or lack of it, feel claustrophobic. He made even Alice feel petite. As he was unable to stand upright in such a low ceilinged cupboard, he signalled her out into the living room. She followed him and they stood together by one of the large sash windows.

'Dr Clarke doesn't seem to have had many neighbours,' he explained. 'The flat below here is unoccupied, it was sold about two months ago, and the basement's occupied by Mr Roberts, a deaf old codger unable to hear his own doorbell. I kept battering at his door until he finally appeared, but it seems he neither saw nor heard anything. Apparently, he hardly knew Elizabeth Clarke anyway, just about enough to say hello on the street. They'd never as much as visited each other's flats.'

'What about No. 2 Bankes Crescent?' Alice asked.

'I checked that out too. It's been divided into student flats and they've all gone home for Christmas. Same with No. 1 Eton Terrace, except for one permanent resident on the second floor, an old lady, a Miss Penrose. I think we should go and speak to her. I've told her what's happened here.'

Miss Penrose's flat was smelly, its air thick with a perfume-mix of wet dog, used cat litter and overcooked cabbage. A dark tunnel of a hall, containing an overflowing cat tray, led to an ill-lit poky sitting room. In among dilapidated pieces of furniture were five small wooden clothes-horses, each laden with a selection of irregularly-shaped bits of towel, dishcloths and strange yellowish undergarments. The only heat in the room came from an old-fashioned one-bar electric heater. Steam was rising from the clothes-horse closest to it and condensed on the tightly snibbed window. Miss Penrose, having welcomed her guests with complete composure, resumed her seat on a shabby, upright armchair with her dog, Piccolo, on her lap. She was stick-thin, with almost translucent skin, and fragile bird-like bones were visible in her tiny, liver-spotted hands. Standing upright she would only be about five foot tall, but she was bent double by osteoporosis, her face now held permanently parallel to the floor. Her sparse white hair revealed expanses of a baby-pink scalp. She was dressed in a strange assortment of hand-knitted things, a tracksuit bottom and an incongruously large pair of blue trainers. In recognition of her company she began to manhandle some cloudy glasses and a decanter on a tray, readying herself to offer sherry.

'No drinks for either of us, but thank you very much. We're on duty,' Alice said, noticing the old lady's crestfallen reaction as with trembling hands she replaced the stopper into the decanter.

'Did you know Dr Clarke?' Alastair asked quickly, as if inquisition was some sort of substitute for conversation.

'Of course I did, quite well. Such a pretty woman. Kind too. She used sometimes to come along for a chat with me. She loved Pico, of course, even though he'd twice tried to bite her. No teeth, fortunately.' She stroked the toothless ball of matted grey fur on her lap, parting its mothy fringe to reveal two little black eyes gleaming malevolently below.

'You'll catch them, eh? He's not much of a guard dog and I'm on my own too... and there'd not be much that I could do.' It was a statement of the obvious; a snail without a shell on a scorching day would have had a better chance of survival.

Alistair nodded, conscious of the thin reassurance, but unable to give more.

'Had you known her long?' he continued.

'Ever since she moved into Bankes Crescent, and that must have been, maybe, ten years or so ago. She used to walk in the gardens, sometimes she even jogged, and that's how I got to know her. Through Pico really. I used to make a lot of my friends through him. But not now, as he can only manage a few yards.'

'Were you at home yesterday evening?'

'Yes, I went to bed early as it was so cold, and I was feeling a bit stiff. Old bones. I fell asleep with the radio on and I didn't wake up until that horrible medley at the end of the World Service transmission. It's at about six am or so. I wasn't aware of anything out of the ordinary until I heard the commotion caused by the arrival of all those police cars.'

'Did you see anyone coming to the door at No. 1 Bankes Crescent yesterday evening?'

'You know, I never saw a thing. I shut my curtains at about five o'clock. I took Pico to the park during the Archers and I was back just before they finished at seven-fifteen pm. Then I took myself off to bed.'

'Can you tell us anything about Elizabeth Clarke?' Alice cut in. 'What sort of person was she?'

Miss Penrose smiled, initially pleased to conjure up the company of her friend.

'She was considerate. A quiet person. At first she was very reserved with me. Many times over the years, when I've been ill, she got my shopping for me. She worked too hard for her own good and I told her so. She was usually back home far too late. I called her Dr Finlay… our joke. She liked a joke. Pico got fond of her, always a good sign, I think. He's a Dandie Dinmont, you know, Kennel-Club registered as "Piccolo Glorious Flute of Liberton", to give him his full name. When my big dog, Dipper, died…'

A single tear trickled down her powdery cheek, to be wiped away discreetly with the side of a finger that carried on in the same movement to tuck a strand of unruly hair back into its clip. Miss Penrose came of a generation reluctant to display deep emotion in front of strangers, believing that if she did so she would be guilty of 'making an exhibition of herself'. The cost of her self-control was more difficult to disguise; a stick-thin knee had begun to shake uncontrollably until she crossed her other leg over it.

'Did Dr Clarke have any family that you know of, Miss Penrose?' Alastair interjected, leading the old lady back to the subject like a dutiful sheepdog with a confused old ewe.

'Her mother's still alive and has a house in East Lothian, Haddington, I think, or maybe Gifford. I'm sure Elizabeth was an only child, like me. She grew up in the country, like me too. Of course, we lived in Lanarkshire in a big house with lots of dogs and even horses. No Dandie Dinmonts though… only fox terriers. Daddy didn't like little dogs, parlour dogs, as he called them. He preferred working dogs, Labradors, fox terriers… even spaniels… now, Tinker…'

Neither sergeant had the heart to cut short Miss Penrose's canine reminiscences too abruptly, so she carried on recalling dead Penrose dogs until, mercifully, her phone rang and they were able to depart, mouthing their gratitude and farewells as she quavered into the receiver.

Alice cradled her coffee mug in her hands as she looked at the typed note from Inspector Manson that lay uppermost on her desk: 'Been to Little France, saw three of Dr Clarke's colleagues in the Obs and Gynae Department, Dr Ian Cross, Dr Robin Maxwell and Dr Kobi al-Alboudie. They say Dr Clarke was ambitious, hard-working and competent. Also "reserved", "independent", "self-contained" and Dr Maxwell says she was a bit "unapproachable". None knew her well enough to know anything about her private life but they all assumed that she was unattached and probably celibate!! I couldn't see Dr Ann Williams, the only other member of the department, she's on annual leave at home. Lives in Drummond Place. Can you go and see her a.s.a.p? You'll probably get more out of her anyway both being professional women, female professionals, whatever!'

Chaos reigned in Ann Williams' kitchen. The floor was covered with a strange assortment of bricks, jigsaw pieces, fridge magnets, crayons and paper. A dog lay chewing the plastic, severed head of a doll, and three little children, two girls and a boy, were standing on stools at the sink, dipping miniature plates and saucers into lathery water with both taps running. 'The Wheels on the Bus' was being belted out by a cassette player in a next door room. Dr Williams left the dicing of carrots, for a chicken stock boiling on the stove, to answer the doorbell.

Alice sat beside her at the table as the woman resumed her chopping, and attempted to concentrate on the task in hand in amongst all the colour, noise and commotion around her. Dr Williams kept her eyes unwaveringly on the children as her knife cut through the carrots, and watching her, Alice half expected to find a severed finger in amongst the heap of prepared vegetables. She began her preamble, but Dr Williams interrupted, explaining, almost impatiently, that she was well aware of her colleague's death as she'd already had news of it from a friend at work. She seemed to understand, without having been told, what was required of her, and began to talk about Elizabeth Clarke unbidden.

'She was an excellent doctor. Not just clever, though she was that too, but compassionate and with a genuine devotion to her work and her patients, or most of them. She was also an ambitious woman... and that doesn't always go down well.' Ann Williams caught Alice's eye, as if to see whether she understood the nature of the unspoken difficulty. Being met with a rueful smile, she went back to her theme: 'She was a bit impatient sometimes, with her less able colleagues I mean, not the patients as far as I am aware. She could seem a bit cool, detached, really, but she wasn't, just completely absorbed in her work. She hated office politics, networking, all those kind of things, even though they are the very kind of things that help on the ascent up the ladder. I think she was generally liked by her subordinates, though she may have intimidated some of them. She did have professional rivals, I suppose I'd be one, but no enemies or anything like that. What else do you need to know?'

'Any boyfriends?'

'Up until about a year ago she was going out with someone called Ian Melville, a painter, an artist or whatever. He lives somewhere out near Leadburn. I only met him twice and, to be frank, I didn't take to him one bit. Arrogant creature. Wrote me off as a philistine when I admitted I'd never heard of someone called Malevich. She's had no one since.'

'Why did they break up?'

A tremendous clattering noise followed immediately by piteous wailing brought the conversation prematurely to an end. One of the little girls had fallen from her stool and lay sprawled on the floor, face downwards and crying. Dr Williams rushed to the fallen child, kissed her injured knee and placed her back on the stool, making soothing noises as she did so. She then rolled up all the children's sleeves before returning to the table.

She repeated the question put to her. 'Why did they break up… Well—', she hesitated, plainly considering whether or not to go on, and then continued, her vegetable knife idle in her hand, '…I think they broke up because Liz had a termination. She didn't tell Ian that she was pregnant until after she had undergone it. That was the end of that. The relationship, I mean. I don't know if he could have forgiven her but she never gave him the chance anyway. The whole thing was a horrible mistake, for both of them probably. I think that she would have broken up with him even if there had been no baby. I never really understood how they got together in the first place, and I was amazed that it lasted as long as it did. Maybe she was just lonely and he was the only port in a storm. He wasn't husband material, or certainly not for her.'

Loud shouts had begun to come from the sink area. The ownership of one of the doll's plates was in dispute. It was being pulled between one of the little girls and her brother. Suddenly his rival let go of the slippery plastic and the boy toppled off his stool onto the floor, clutching his prize. The impact was accompanied by a loud crack, and then full-lunged crying.

'Jesus Christ!' Dr Williams muttered, briefly rubbing her eyes with her hands before sighing loudly and rising to tend to the child. As she was doing so his sister coolly got off her stool and took the plate from beside him as he lay there. A new chorus of 'Three Little Monkeys' started up on the cassette, and Alice decided, without regret, that the time to leave the scene of controlled chaos had arrived.

Dr Clarke's mother had been tracked down to an address in Haddington, and the two Detective Sergeants travelled there together in a white Astra from the pool. The woman lived in the Sidegate, in a perfect little Georgian doll's house in a terrace of such houses. Mrs Clarke, on first seeing the place over eleven years ago, had determined that this was to be her final home, a house that she would exit from feet first only. It was close to Elizabeth, close to St Mary's, close to the River Tyne, and if she had to live on cardboard for the rest of her life to get it, then so be it. It would be worth it. The quiet little market town of Haddington suited her needs well, being big enough to host a decent choir but small enough for the locals to be recognised by the shopkeepers, even at the check-out in the supermarket. She had never contemplated life there all on her own, without her daughter nearby. Elizabeth was never ill, had never as much as broken a bone in her body, and was over thirty years younger than her. Why should she?

She knew the police were coming, knew as a result of the telephone call why they were coming. Somehow she had managed not to collapse on seeing her only child, Elizabeth, dead, laid out on a cold, mortuary table. She repeated the words in her head ,'Elizabeth. Dead.', as if by doing so she would rob them of meaning or make them untrue or, at the very least, accustom herself to their import. The jangling of her nerves as the doorbell rang reminded her, as if she needed it, of the intense emotional state she was in, although, so far, she had managed externally to conceal it. Composure mattered. If you seemed to be in control then, to all intents and purposes, you were in control and, at times like this, control was paramount. She showed the two sergeants into her drawing room, noticing, as she did so, that the poinsettia in the alcove seemed to have dried out, its red leaves tinged with brown. Her offer of tea was declined and Mrs Clarke began to speak about her child, fastidiously correcting her tenses to reflect the death of her daughter.

'Elizabeth's a very… she was a very thoughtful person. I was lucky to have her as a daughter. My husband died when she was only seven, so there were just the two of us. She always tried to make me proud of her. And I was… and I am. She was doing very well and she loves her job at the Infirmary… loved… the job. I don't see what else I can tell you…' Her voice began to peter out, and Alice, sensing that if the old lady stopped altogether, she might be unable to hold on to her composure, quickly tried a new topic.

'I understand that Elizabeth went out with a man called Ian Melville?'

'Yes,' Mrs Clarke nodded, 'she was fond of Ian. So was I. I was very sorry when it all came to an end.' An expression of acute pain suddenly transformed the woman's previously impassive features, 'Oh God!' she exclaimed, tears beginning to stream down her pale cheeks, '…if only she'd kept the child, their child, I'd have a little of her left. Something of her. She should never have had that abortion, I never approved. Never approved. We are Catholics, so was Ian. I suppose she knew what I'd say, what he'd have said…'

The full realisation of her double loss was too much, and she covered her face with her hands, sobbing uncontrollably, oblivious now to the strangers by her side.

3

Monday 5th December

Sammy McBryde's right hand landed, with a thud, on the top of the alarm clock, silencing it with one decisive blow. He yawned and stretched, before ruffling his tousled black curls with his fingers and scratching his scalp. In slow motion, he manoeuvred himself out of bed, trying not to disturb his still-sleeping girlfriend, and wandered into the kitchen in his T-shirt and pants to make their morning tea. By the time he returned, Shona's eyes were open and he passed a chipped mug, silently, to her. Conversation before breakfast usually degenerated into argument, and they had both independently concluded that wordless communication was preferable to the daily bickering that had preceded it. They lay together, thighs just touching, relishing the first and best cup of the day, until Sammy, mug now drained, lit up a cigarette and passed the packet on to his companion. He took a deep drag, steeled himself to leave the comforting warmth of the bed, flung back the bedclothes and raced to their damp, unheated bathroom.

All of yesterday's clothing lay in a muddled heap on the floor, a black bra snaked across the woolly bathmat and a pair of laddered tights lay, in the missionary position, on rumpled blue jeans. He extracted his work clothes as quickly as possible, noticing the goose pimples on his naked arms, and dressed in haste, rejecting only a jersey stiff with mud from the previous day's work. The jeans would last one more day, they didn't actually smell yet. Shona's eyes were closed when he kissed her goodbye, brushing her cheek with his lips and delighting in the warmth and smooth texture of her skin. He double-locked the front door on the way out, feeling like a sultan protecting the treasure contained within.

The minute he stepped beyond the shelter of the porch he was assaulted by driving rain, blowing horizontally at him and turning the gutters into fast-flowing burns. He began to run, head bowed, through the downpour, splashing and soaking his trousers with every step, until he reached his battered old van. The pockets of his wet jeans stuck to his thighs, making it difficult for his cold hands to get a grip of the keys inside, never mind extract them. The van started, coughing thickly like an old smoker, and he rattled down the Medway in it towards Granton Road.

Davie was waiting for him huddled against the cold and rain, getting whatever inadequate shelter he could beneath the flapping awning of a grocer's shop. He stank of rum, and his thick, tobacco stained fingers were clamped around a damp little roll-up. That the old fellow continued to cling onto life was, in itself, miraculous. He worked every day, Saturdays and Sundays included, often in the cold and wet, got the cash in hand he required and immediately converted it into rum at the Tarbat Inn. Any cheques he deigned to accept had to be made out to his drinking house, as it was also his bank. The state remained blissfully unaware of his existence: he claimed no benefits, paid no taxes and elected to cast no vote. Solid food, bar the odd pork chop grilled at midnight, rarely passed his lips, and he slept only for a few hours every evening. The remainder of the night was spent sitting upright in an armchair reading, devouring anything and everything in print, feasting equally happily on cowboy novels or cookery books.

As Davie hauled himself up into the van, Sammy noticed for the first time that the old fellow's pale, cracked lips appeared to be tinged with blue, and his curranty eyes, largely obscured by his woolly bonnet, seemed duller than usual. Davie was the brains behind their partnership. The pair hired themselves out as jobbing gardeners, but they would turn their hands to whatever manual labour was requested by those desperate enough to employ them. Davie's ability to work out the exact materials required for any job was prodigious, accurate to the last brick or nail, and none of their hard-earned profit was wasted on excess materials. Naturally, he paid himself an extra pound an hour out of their joint wage for his own managerial skills, and this was alright by Sammy; he wanted no responsibility anyway.

The van entered the leafy environs of Primrose Bank as the sun began to emerge from behind black, lowering clouds, and the rain dwindled into little more than drizzle before stopping altogether. They spent the morning, in their soggy clothes, laying sand and slabs for a frosty widow who monitored their every move from behind her net curtains, and remonstrated with them when they stopped, for ten minutes, for a tea break. Not on my time, if you please.

At twelve o'clock precisely they were paid in cash, as previously agreed, and rumbled off in the van along the glistening roads to the Tarbat for the first of Davie's rums for the day. Sammy sat in the motor in the pub car park, eating the cheese sandwiches he'd made the night before and reading *Principles of Practical Beekeeping*, a good introduction to his new hobby. Tropical fish were too expensive nowadays, always dying and developing untreatable diseases. Anyway, he'd left the aquarium behind in the old flat, with his old life, and bees at least produced something, even if their stings might take a little getting used to. One day, one day soon, he and Shona would move into the country, somewhere on the Lammermuirs maybe, and she'd have her bed and breakfast and he'd keep bees.

'When mating occurs, the drone not only gives the queen his passionate embrace, but also his life. The male organs are detached during coupling, the drone dying almost immediately and the queen returns to her hive with the proof of her meeting firmly implanted in her body.'

Involuntarily his mind flashed from bees to humans, and he stopped chewing his bread, almost choking on it at the sickening image suddenly and graphically appearing before his eyes. The unpleasant picture was dispelled by the sound of Davie rapping cheerily on the driver's side window, signalling that their lunch hour was all but over. They travelled back to Primrose Bank in silence, Sammy trying to focus his mind on the site of his hives in the heather at Kidlaw and Davie busily calculating the number of slabs required for the spiral finish that the widow wanted near her pond.

The sound of the wheelbarrow tipping over, the bricks inside clattering onto the gravel path, alerted Sammy to Davie's collapse. The old man lay on the grass, one leg trapped beneath the still half-full barrow. His eyes were closed, cap askew and he seemed to have wet himself. Sammy called his name, even slapped him lightly on the face as he'd seen done on television, but was unable to rouse his partner. He ran to the widow's door and hammered on it. The door opened abruptly, and the woman stared at him as if he had no idea of his place and needed an immediate, unspoken reminder.

'It's ma pal, Davie, he's collapsed. Ye'll need tae phone fir an ambulance...'

Despite the entreaty in his voice her reply was cold.

'Have you not got a mobile telephone like everyone else?'

For Sammy, patience was a commodity in short supply at the best of times, and the only explanation necessary had already been provided.

'Fer fuck's sake woman, jist phone the hospital will ye? I'll need tae move him in here, oot o' the rain. It's pissin' doon oan him.' He turned round as if to go and collect the body, muttering obscenities at her under his breath.

'Just a minute, if you don't mind. I'd rather you just took him to the shed, he'll be under shelter there. I don't know either of you from Adam, and the box's full of scare stories about ruses for getting into peoples houses… em… I'm not suggesting you… but all the same… I'd rather…'

'Away tae fuck wi' ye.'

By the time Sammy returned to Davy's prostrate body, little moans were coming from his sodden form, and saliva appeared to be bubbling out of his mouth.

The ambulancemen were gentle, easing the slight body onto a stretcher and picking up the loose change as it fell from his pockets onto the soaked ground. Sammy knew he should tell them that Davie was an alcoholic. Even if he recovered he'd soon start suffering the DTs and it would be all too obvious. But he didn't like to betray his friend, and if he did they might try to involve him in some way. Instead, he gave the men the old fellow's address and provided a false one for himself, otherwise they might try to contact him to help with any recuperation or, God forbid, arrangements for a funeral, and, really, it was none of his business. Davie had a missus somewhere, shed years ago, but no doubt the authorities would be able, somehow, to contact her.

Sammy let himself into the house, luxuriating in its empty state, the welcome absence of any sulky wife, noisy children or screaming babies. Soon the taps were on, filling the pink bathtub and warming the cool air of the bathroom with steam. Soft music on the radio soothed him as he lay in the hot water, secure in the knowledge that no one was impatiently waiting to take his place, Shona would not be returning from her work as a barmaid until at least eleven-thirty pm. He had a good six hours all to himself. He washed his hair with her coconut-scented shampoo and scrubbed his fingernails vigorously to remove all the day's grime. Looking around him he saw that all the clothing which had previously littered the floor had gone, and that Shona had laid out clean clothes for him on the bathroom chair. The ironed pile included the raspberry pink shirt, chosen by her before she understood his tastes, but no-one would see him in it in the house. Dressing, he felt an animal pleasure in his cleanliness, with the sweet smell of soap on his body and his crisp, freshly laundered kit.

In the kitchen he unwrapped the parcel of fish and chips that had been keeping warm in its brown paper in the oven. The hiss of the ring-pull on the Tennants can made for the perfect evening. He opened *Principles of Practical Beekeeping* and read on:

'Towards the end of summer, rearing and mating of queens usually ceases and as a colony has no further use for its now redundant residents, the workers turn upon the drones in fury. First they gnaw their wing bases so that they are unable to fly, then forcibly eject them from their home, where they quickly perish from cold…'.

He thanked God that he hadn't been born a bee, and closed the book hurriedly. Perhaps the TV would make for the truly perfect evening, so he flicked on the remote and was heartened to see the rugged features of Steve McQueen contort as he punched a cop on the jaw. Just as he felt himself slumping a few inches further into the easy chair he heard a knock on his front door. Steve was just about to land another punch, this time to the cop's eye, so for a moment he considered ignoring the caller, but he had never been able to let a phone ring unanswered or disregard a doorbell. You never knew when such things might not signal an emergency: Shona might have been hurt or something. He pulled himself, reluctantly, to his feet, took a final swig of his lager and went to see who had come to call.

4

Tuesday 6th December
DCI Bell waited impatiently for the rump of her squad to arrive. Eric Manson breezed in, last of all, as if he was attending a social gathering of some sort, clutching his polystyrene mug of coffee and nodding to his pals as he found his way to his seat.

'Are you quite ready, Eric?' Elaine Bell asked sarcastically.

'Sorry Ma'am, got held up in the traffic,' Eric replied, apparently uncontrite.

'When I say nine, I mean nine. Nine o'clock precisely.' She continued, unpleasantly aware that she sounded like an exasperated primary school teacher.

'Last night a man named Samuel McBryde was found murdered in his home at Granton Medway. He was aged thirty-six and was discovered by his girlfriend, Shona Gordon, when she returned to their home after her work. She reckons it was at about eleven-fifty pm. His throat had been cut, and the pathologists think that the killing took place earlier that evening, which accords with the information we have from the girlfriend that McBryde normally got back home at about five or five-thirty pm. Another bit of lined paper, this time with the word "worthless", and again written in green ink, was present near the victim's left foot.' She cleared her throat, before carrying on:

'It looks like whoever was responsible for Dr Clarke's death also killed Samuel McBryde. In both cases, the initial incision was high up on the left side of the neck, starting from just below the ear. Anyway, the presence of the pieces of paper with their inscriptions can hardly be coincidence. But Christ alone knows what the connection between the two of them is. Dr Clarke's cleaner doesn't think any knives were missing from the doctor's flat. Miss Gordon doesn't think that anything's been taken from their house, two twenty-pound notes were lying on the kitchen table untouched. Neither she nor Mr McBryde were drug users...'

Manson interrupted, 'Is that on Miss Gordon's say-so, boss? She's hardly likely to admit that they were users to us.'

'Yes, Eric. It's on Miss Gordon's say-so and I'm quite aware of the likely reliability of any such statements. If I could continue?' She shot an impatient glance at the Detective Inspector before resuming her address, 'As before, there were no signs of forced entry, so it seems probable that both victims knew their killer. In the circumstances, it's been decided to enlarge the Murder Squad and we are to be assisted by some of the Leith people. We are getting DSs Moray and Sands and DCs Porter and Lindsay. The scene of crime officers are already at the locus...'

DCI Bell allocated the day's tasks amongst the squad. Alice was assigned, with Alastair, to talk to McBryde's neighbours in Granton Medway. The place, when they eventually found it, was a midden, about as far removed from the graceful Georgian architecture of the New Town as a pygmy village on the Congo. Two rows of bleak, cement-harled houses were separated by a road rutted with potholes and pavements blotched with different shades of tarmac grey, a patchwork of repairs. Squat wheelie-bins flanked each communal doorway, many of them displaying obscenities in thick white paint. Litter was strewn everywhere as if a vast bin had exploded in the centre of the estate, showering everything in it over the houses, including the ubiquitous satellite dishes. The houses on either side of McBryde's had their windows boarded up and then, for additional security, metal shutters had been fitted.

In such a place the presence of any stranger was a cause for concern amongst the residents: bound to be a rent man, a bailiff, a DSS snoop or a vandal. The police were as unwelcome as the rest of them, nowhere to be seen when help was needed but ever-present when they wanted some. Eternal vigilance was the key to survival in the Medway, and the leisure provided by unemployment meant a full complement of sentries in the dwellings still occupied. The two sergeants trekked dutifully from door to door, hunched against the cold rain, avoiding the dog mess and broken glass, only to be told again and again that nothing had been seen, nothing had been heard. One inhabitant, among the hundreds, was prepared to co-operate, but then just to volunteer that Sammy had returned home in his van at about five pm.

If the tourists visiting Holyrood Palace and Charlotte Square considered the capital akin to a beautiful woman, elegant and well-coiffeured, then Granton Medway was her underwear, and none too clean at that. It was a place forsaken by God and man alike, one where the few residents that remained shared a single, burning ambition, to move somewhere—anywhere—else.

Dr Clarke's former boyfriend, Ian Melville, was waiting in an interview room at St Leonard's when they returned, weary and dispirited from the palpable antagonism that had met them in Granton. He'd been traced by DC Porter to an address in the city, St Bernard's Row in Stockbridge, having left Leadburn about a month earlier. The man was tall, well over six feet, with long, gangly limbs and oversized hands and feet. He had the sort of irregular, asymmetrical features which produce either a plug-ugly face or one of great attraction, with deep-set dark eyes, a hook of a nose and crooked, inward-leaning teeth. The combination in his case was arresting, eye-catching in its idiosyncratic appeal. As they entered, Alice saw him remove his drumming fingers from the table onto his trousers, where they continued, hidden, to drum on his thighs. Neither sergeant subscribed to the nasty-nice school of interrogation, preferring instead the role of overworked schoolteachers whose patience should not be stretched beyond its limit, for fear of some unspoken repercussion. As a tactic it often worked well, somehow regressing the interviewees back to powerless schoolchildren facing some omnipotent dominie from their past. The truly recalcitrant were left to Eric Manson and his incoherent code of ethics.

'You'll be aware, Mr Melville, of the death of Dr Elizabeth Clarke,' Alice began.

'I read the papers like everyone else, yes.'

'Can you tell me where you were between five pm on Thursday evening and nine pm the next morning?'

'Am I a suspect?' Melville asked defensively.

'No. You're simply assisting us with our enquiries. Is that alright with you?'

The man hesitated before replying, 'Fine.' His anxious expression undermined his words.

'So can you tell me where you were…'

'On Thursday evening I worked in my studio until about eight or so, and then I went home.'

'Where is your studio?'

'In Stockbridge, Henderson Row.'

'Stockbridge. Anyone see you at your studio?'

'I don't know. I certainly didn't see anyone else there. Does that matter? I can show you the work that I was doing if necessary.'

'After leaving the studio you walked home to St Bernard's Row?'

'Yes. I collected a carry-out from the Chinese and spent the rest of the evening in, watching the television, until I went to bed.'

'Were you on your own all the time?'

'Yes, but I have no one to confirm I was actually there, if that's what you're getting at.'

'Any phone calls to you or made by you?'

'No. I don't think so. I use a mobile anyway.'

'What did you watch on TV?'

'I can't remember now. I think I watched a DVD, something I'd got from the shop.'

Alastair decided that his turn had come, and catching Alice's eye, cut in.

'I understand that you and Dr Clarke went out with each other up until about a year ago?'

'That's correct.'

'Why did the relationship end?'

Melville didn't answer immediately. He looked at his interrogators keenly, as if trying to assess what they might already know, and then committed himself.

'You already know the cause, I'd guess. We broke up as Liz decided to have a termination, as she called it—an abortion, to have our child aborted.'

'You hadn't agreed to this?'

'I wasn't consulted. I was presented with a *fait accompli*.'

'Had you been aware that Dr Clarke was pregnant?'

'No.'

'If you'd been told, what would your reaction have been?'

'I'd have been delighted. What can I say? I loved Liz, I would have wanted my child to be half her, Liz to be the mother of my children.'

'So you would have tried to stop her having an abortion?'

'Obviously, if I had known.'

'And you're a Catholic?'

'Lapsed. A lapsed Catholic.'

'What was your reaction when you heard what she'd done?'

Melville's expression changed to one of hostility, disbelief that such a stupid question could be uttered. What the hell would you feel if your baby had been killed? When, at last, he spoke, he spoke slowly.

'At first I didn't believe her… I couldn't believe it. But it's not the kind of thing you make up, is it? So when the news sank in I was… furious, disgusted, sad… appalled. We had a tremendous row.'

'Disgusted?' Alice asked.

'Disgusted with her. I never thought she could do such a thing, not her. It made me think of her differently—she had killed our child.'

'Who ended the relationship?' she continued.

'She did… Liz did. After the row she refused my calls, never answered my letters, and on the one occasion when I waited for her to return to Bankes Crescent from work, she cut me dead, wouldn't say a word and shut the front door in my face.'

'Have you had any girlfriends since Dr Clarke?'

His hackles rose again. None of your business.

'No, I haven't even been looking. I told you, I loved her and it's not easy to get someone like that out of your system, even after what she did.'

Alastair showed Melville a photo of Sammy McBryde. 'Do you know him?'

'Never seen him in my life before.'

'Can you tell us where you were yesterday evening between four-thirty pm and, say, eleven-fifty pm?'

'I worked in my studio until about eight pm or so, then I met a pal, Roddy, for a drink at the Raeburn Inn. I left there at about ten, I think, and went home. It's just round the corner from the pub. I watched the TV until I went to bed.'

'Anyone at home with you? Any calls?'

'No. I can't prove that I was there, but I was.'

'Can you give us Roddy's full name and address?'

'Roderick Cohen, St Stephen's Street. I'll get the flat number.'

No one brushed the stairs within Alice's tenement in Broughton Place; they belonged to everyone in the block and so were cleaned by nobody. The last time they'd been swept was when one of the flats was for sale; a potential purchaser could not be expected to overlook the squalor routinely disregarded by the residents.

Alice trudged upwards, blind as ever to the dust, stopping only when she reached Miss Spinell's flat on the second floor. Without the aged spinster's help as a dog-sitter she would have been unable to keep Quill, her collie cross mongrel, and she was painfully aware of her dependence on the animal for company, a source of silent support and uncritical adoration, and on Miss Spinell's goodwill as his daytime keeper. Fortunately, the old lady needed the dog as much, if not more, than Alice, as in his absence day after endless day would be spent alone behind the multiple mortice and Yale locks with which she fortified her front door. Alzheimer's was creeping up on her in the form of a thief, a thief who made free with the contents of her fridge, her pan cupboard and her underwear drawers. One day her favourite aluminium cooking pot would have disappeared, the next a tin of sockeye salmon would appear half-consumed beside the ice cubes, and her numerous locks no longer provided any protection against the quick-fingered scoundrel.

Alice knocked on the heavy door and waited patiently for the characteristic thuds, clicks and bangs which always preceded its opening. Finally, her identity having been confirmed from behind the last chain, Quill was released to her with the usual polite little nod that signalled the changeover of custody. The dog ran, yelping excitedly, up to their flat on the third floor and waited patiently as Alice fished in her bag for her keys. As the door swung open, she caught the end of a message on her answerphone. Bridget's voice: 'Sorry you're not in. Had thought we might meet up tonight. I'll try again later in the week.'

She breathed a sigh of relief. No white lies needed to excuse her reluctance to leave home again, just the prospect of a drink in the company of her own thoughts. She poured herself a glass of New Zealand white, unable, as she sipped it slowly, to switch off. Ian Melville seemed believable, but he had a motive or two for killing his former lover, and the opportunity; his house and studio were less than ten minutes from the victim's flat. Of course, he had no alibi, but he seemed, somehow, an unlikely killer. Surely, if he had done it, it would have been in the heat of the moment, a crime of passion. Yet Dr Clarke's cleaner said that no knives were missing, which meant the murderer must have brought his own blade with him. So it must have been a premeditated crime, just like Sammy McBryde's. The paper chase connecting the killings and the calculated way in which they had been carried out were as if someone wanted to ensure that they got the credit for both.

5

Joe used to marvel that she slept so peacefully, motionless with her head invariably turned to the left. Like she was already dead, he'd once observed. Not tonight, though. Alice could not keep still, she could feel herself tossing and turning, now one arm above her head, now to the side, now one hand under the covers, now on top. No position was comfortable, no position brought sleep any closer. The sheets themselves seemed to be made of sandpaper, abrading her face and bare arms. She needed to talk to someone, to unburden her mind of the thoughts that were chasing each other, exhausting her. Two am. But there were no friends good enough for that any more, and no lover to be roused in extremis like this. If Joe had been beside her she could have touched his shoulder or whispered his name, confided in him the troubles that now wracked her. But he was the trouble, or a big part of it, the one who had explained that dependence was attractive, that independence was not always viewed as a virtue in women. It was Joe who had planted the seed of doubt in her mind, now a full-canopied tree, and then gone away. At four am Alice gave up the unequal struggle, turned on the light and finished the bottle of wine in the fridge. If nothing else could bring about slumber, alcohol certainly would, even if her return to consciousness would be accompanied by a hammer and anvil of a headache.

She woke four hours later, unrefreshed, nauseous and feeling that her age had doubled overnight. Her bedroom mirror, ruthless in its honesty, reflected a sallow-skinned, red-eyed stranger sitting up in her bed. Quill slipped off his chair in one fluid movement, stretched, wagged his tail and bounded, bright-eyed, into the kitchen as if it was the first morning of creation. He knew the routine, and in anticipation of his walk raced round the flat while his mistress dressed with care, preparing herself for the cold world outside—the cold, still dark, world. Twenty minutes later the pair set off towards Canonmills, the dog straining on the lead, pulling his reluctant owner with him from lamppost to lamppost, zigzagging all the way to the park.

Alastair was already at his desk by half past eight, phone clamped to his ear, when Alice arrived at the station. He looked her up and down and then scribbled a note, displaying it to her as he continued to speak into the receiver.

'ROUGH NIGHT, EH?' She nodded meekly, preferring the picture of her carousing with friends until the early hours to any explanation, or exploration, of the real cause of her sleeplessness. Eric Manson approached their desks and then, on seeing her, started back theatrically as if encountering some horrible vision. She could not be bothered to smile but managed to manufacture a weak rictus, sufficient to communicate her appreciation of his tired joke and send him, contented, on his way. The blacksmith in her head had begun to pound away again, blow after blow to the left temple, undeterred by the aspirin she'd forced down with her coffee. Another sleepless night, another ruined day, and all because Joe could not handle her as she was, as she wanted to be. And now the sod was even muscling in on her waking hours, not content with destroying her nights.

'That was a Mr Burns,' Alastair said, interrupting his companion's thoughts. 'He lives in Lennox Street and has just returned from holiday. He saw a report about Dr Clarke's death in the *Evening News* and has remembered that on the night of the killing he saw a group of three people, a man and two women, patrolling the area. Lennox Street is no distance from Bankes Crescent. We'd better go and speak to him.'

The Burns' house presented a neat exterior to the neighbourhood: trimmed hedge, gravelled path and a garden bereft of flowers and weeds. The cement patio that had replaced the lawn sported a collection of brightly coloured, glazed pots, each containing tufts of dry grasses or other architectural plants. Jack Burns had no time for cultivation, he was a golfing man and his home was a shrine dedicated to the ancient sport, hung with tinted prints of its holy places, St Andrews and Muirfield, and bedecked with glistening trophies, usually depicting rigid figures in plus fours swinging clubs. He exuded confidence, the confidence of the law- abiding citizen who has no concern about faulty tail-lights or an out-of-date tax disc. For him the police were simply public servants employed to assist righteous taxpayers, like himself, in their eternal struggle against the great unwashed. As Alice and Alastair took their seats in the immaculate sitting room, Mrs Burns, a timid, downtrodden-looking creature, entered bearing a tray laden with fine china, tea and biscuits for the guests. She lowered her load onto the coffee table nervously, looked up at her husband and was dismissed, with a grimace, from the meeting.

'Could you describe for us the individuals that you saw?' Alastair began.

'As I said on the phone, Officer, a man and two women. I saw them as I was parking the car. They all appeared respectable, the man in a suit and tie and the ladies both in skirts and car coats.' Mr Burns' voice was surprisingly high, almost a treble. Alice had expected a baritone to come from the corpulent man. His intonation betrayed his Morningside origins, no need to conceal them in the West End.

'Can you give us any clue as to their ages?' Alastair asked.

'I didn't get a close view, but middle-aged, I'd say.'

'What were they doing?'

'I only saw them for a minute, if that. They were calling at my neighbours, the Osbornes, and getting no answer they moved to the next house, Mrs Morris's. No Mr Morris now, if there ever was, and frankly I doubt it. She let them in. They were all back in the street about forty minutes later. I had to collect something from my car which was parked outside our house.'

'What time was it when you first saw them?'

'I'd just got back from work, so maybe six-thirty pm.'

'So when you went out to your car later, it would be about seven-ten or seven-twenty, something like that?'

'Yes, that's correct, Officer.'

'What were they doing then?'

'They were knocking on someone else's door.'

'Whose door?'

'Mrs Jarvis's, but they'd have no luck there whatever they were up to.' Mr Burns pursed his lips, blatantly inviting further questions.

'Oh?' Alice enquired, an unwilling participant in the man's breathless game.

'Another neurotic female. Her husband left her about a year ago for a younger model, and no surprise there since she'd let herself go completely, no face-paint whatsoever and she lived in trousers. Since he left she's become a virtual recluse, peering out of her curtains occasionally, but no one darkens her door except her son, poor brute. His life's not his own any more. No chance of any strangers being allowed over that threshold.'

If like-minded people are attracted to the same places, then Mrs Morris had no business living in Lennox Street. She answered the door clad in a paint-streaked boiler suit and old plimsolls, the whole ensemble being set off by a peroxide-blond crew cut.

In the privacy of her studio she explained that the three visitors had been Jehovah's Witnesses, intent upon converting her until she had explained to them that she was a practising Nichiren Buddhist, evangelical in her own way, and currently engaged on a thesis entitled 'The History of the Lotus Sutra'. Their departure had been hastened by her offer to teach them a chant central to her belief, and she laughed out loud remembering the alacrity with which they collected their umbrellas, pamphlets and papers as soon as she began to intone 'Nam myok…'.

The sergeants were greeted like old friends by the Jehovah's Witnesses at the nearby Kingdom Hall. Followers appeared from nowhere, men and women, old and young, all smiling kindly at them and one bearing refreshments. They were led, superflous mugs of tea in hand, to a comfortable seating area, a space reserved for leather-covered armchairs and long, low tables covered in brightly coloured little books and pamphlets. Their escorts mysteriously drifted away, but one old lady remained with them, sipping her tea companionably and radiating a benign contentment at their appearance. Alice, realising that the Witnesses believed that their visit was due to a desire for conversion or, at the very least, further information leading to conversion, drew her identity card from her pocket and showed it to their hostess. The effect was immediate, and the old lady's expression changed into one of anxiety.

'How can we help you, Officers?' she said.

'We would like to speak, if possible, to any of the three Witnesses who were in Lennox Street last Thursday evening,' Alice replied.

The old lady blinked nervously, and then bellowed, with surprising vigour, 'Eva! Eva! Come out here.'

The mousy woman who had distributed the tea emerged from behind a partially open door and joined them in the seating area. A lifetime of knocking on strangers' doors and being met with abuse had prepared her for any ordeal, and an interview with the police was as nothing compared to one night's evangelising in the rougher parts of Midlothian, places where gobs of spittle often accompanied the slamming of doors. In response to their polite inquiries she explained that neither she, nor either of the others, had seen anything unusual that evening. They had, indeed, called at No. 1 Bankes Crescent. It was the last house they'd tried before thankfully abandoning their night's chore and returning to the hall, weighed down with as many leaflets as they'd set out with. It had been a bad shift, with little kindness from any quarter, and they were all too disheartened to continue trying to spread the word any longer. She reckoned that they'd been at Dr Clarke's front door at about nine pm and had got no response from any of the three flats.

As Eva began to describe their cool reception earlier that evening in Lennox Street, Alice's mind drifted back to the information they'd already obtained, automatically assessing its import. The trio had been in and out of other people's houses throughout the evening, so they could easily have missed all, or any, significant movements for the whole time. However, Dr Clarke had not responded when they had pressed her bell. She would not have been able to see who was at the front door from her flat, and medics couldn't ignore callers as their services might be needed. Anyway, Dr Clarke was probably too polite, or too curious, to allow a doorbell to ring without responding to it in some way. So by nine pm she was probably dead.

DI Eric Manson had a gift, an unusual one, a gift for annoying Alice beyond endurance, and since he had discovered this particular accomplishment he had enjoyed exercising it to the full.

'Ian Melville killed Dr Clarke, mark my words, Alice. He was turned down by her again and couldn't accept it.'

'No, Sir, I don't think so,' she replied in measured tones.

'Face it, love, he had a motive and he had the opportunity. She'd spurned him, killed his kid, for Christ's sake, what more do you want? Just because he's good-looking, maybe even available...' The caress of the flame on the blue touchpaper had been too close, and Alice's response was immediate and heated.

'His good looks, as you call them, Sir, have nothing to do with anything. Everyone who ends a relationship isn't killed, everyone who refuses to re-ignite a relationship doesn't have their throat slit. Abortions are performed every day and the mothers don't end up in the mortuary. What we have on Melville, at the moment, all that we have, is his historic relationship with Dr Clarke, the proximity of their addresses and the absence of any alibi for the time at which she was probably killed.'

'That's what you think,' Manson said provocatively, adding, with mock disbelief, 'and as if that's not enough!'

Alice and Alastair exchanged glances. Manson was well known for preferring to play with his own hand-picked team, and neither of them were under any illusion that they'd figure even as reserves if he had his way. It would not be the first time that he had been deliberately slow in exchanging intelligence crucial to the team as a whole. Fortunately, he was deprived of the opportunity of flourishing his additional information to maximum dramatic effect by the entry of DC Lindsay, announcing that a squad meeting had been called.

While surveying those assembled in the room DCI Bell crunched her cough sweet, menthol fumes invading her sinuses and making her blink repeatedly. Her voice was hoarse from a heavy cold, and she still looked colourless and panda-eyed. She should have been tucked up in bed asleep, not addressing her troops.

'Listen up, please, as they say in the movies. We need to consider where we are in this investigation and where we're going. Considering first Dr Clarke. We've just heard from the fingerprint boys that prints, matching those of Ian Melville, have been found on a glass taken from Dr Clarke's kitchen.' Alice became aware that Manson was smirking at her, so she continued to stare impassively at her boss.

'We know he had a motive for the killing,' Elaine Bell rasped painfully on, 'and there's no one to vouch for his whereabouts on the night in question. He made no mention to Alice or Alastair of any recent visit to Dr Clarke, so I want him questioned again.' The DCI looked at her two sergeants to check that her orders had been understood, before continuing, 'So far the doctor's neighbours have been of little help, but the stuff provided by the Jehovah's Witnesses may suggest that by nine pm or thereabouts she was already dead. That would accord, roughly, with the pathologist's opinion about the time of death. We're no further on in relation to the scraps of paper, and we've still no murder weapon. Eric's got nothing so far from his extended interviews with the doctor's colleagues…'.

'I'm due to see Dr Ferguson about now, Ma'am,' Manson interjected, rising as he spoke.

'Off you go then, Eric,' Bell whispered. She cleared her throat, tried to speak and then cleared it again, making her voice no more audible.

'We've got a set of matching prints from Dr Clarke's flat,' she croaked, 'and Granton Medway. A set over and above those left by Melville in Dr Clarke's flat. The unidentified ones are no real surprise given the killer's calling cards. McBryde's neighbours haven't provided anything useful and the search is still on around the Medway for the weapon.' DCI Bell's voice tailed off completely. She made one more attempt to speak before whispering 'I'm sorry, I can't go on. Can you allocate everyone else their duties, Sandy?'

'Aye.' DS Moray assented.

Back in the office Alastair phoned Ian Melville's home number and got a woman's voice, upper class and assured. It told him that Melville was away in London. No, she didn't know where. No, she couldn't contact him on his mobile as he'd bought a new one and she didn't have the number. All she could tell them was that he was supposed to be coming back to the flat on Thursday evening. If they wanted to see him again they would have to wait until then.

6

Wednesday 7th December

Cycling up the Mound in winter was a bad idea. The chilly inhaled air hurt the lungs, and the heavy tweed overcoat meant added weight. David Pearson QC climbed off his large black lady's bicycle and began to push it. Honour had been satisfied, he'd managed to stay in the saddle and propel the thing until he was opposite the Playfair Steps. On reaching Parliament House he rested it against one of the pillars flanking the entrance to Court No. 11 and entered the building via the men's gown room. He changed into his court dress, noticing, as he did so, a grimy stain on his fall, and made a mental note to get another one from the laundry next week. How efficient he had been, buying one of his wife's Christmas presents, a huge bottle of Jo Malone Grapefruit bath oil, and all before his court day had even begun. She'd be touched that he'd remembered her favourite essence.

He collected his papers for the Proof, hitched his creased gown up onto his shoulders and set off for the reading room. With the enhanced powers of observation that adrenaline seemed to give him, he noticed his opponent, Angus Goode QC, sitting at the window closest to the portrait of the late Lord Justice-Clerk. Goode was an aggressive maverick but, unfortunately, no fool, invariably difficult to deal with, playing his cards so close to his chest that they should have become entangled in his body hair, and displaying an unhealthy appetite for a courtroom scrap. Pearson poured himself a cup of black coffee but felt, as he'd expected, too nauseous to drink it. That Islay malt would be his undoing. A digestive biscuit remained dry in his mouth, and he finally put it back on the plate after only one bite. Some sugar would be essential for the forthcoming fray. Fortunately he'd stowed some chocolate in his pocket, and he'd force himself to get a few squares of that down before he was required to perform. He looked, for the tenth time, at the Closed Record, and then moved on to the plethora of contradictory expert reports. Plainly, the pursuer was a liar or 'a stranger to the truth', as he would submit. Sufficient evidence existed, if properly presented, to establish that to any sane judge's satisfaction, and, please God, his Lord Ordinary would fall into that category.

His uneasy contemplation was disturbed by his Junior, Rowena Fox, taking the seat opposite. It was odd, he was the Senior, and yet in her presence he felt the inferior. She smiled at him in her cool, efficient way, but she had miscalculated; he wasn't one of her conquests, having always been entirely immune to her glacial charms. A hair out of place would have been an improvement as far as he was concerned. He could sense that she was itching to discuss the case, to give him the benefit of her views, but the thought was repellent to him, he felt queasy enough already. Inspiration came to him, and he sent her off to photocopy the first case that came into his head, knowing it had no relevance whatsoever to the day's business but was thirty pages long at least. As soon as Miss Fox, or 'The Vixen' as he preferred to call her, had left her seat it was taken by Goode, and it was obvious that he wanted to negotiate.

'Any offers to be made this morning?' he enquired casually.

Pearson looked his opponent straight in the eye as he replied, 'Nuisance value at most, and I'm not even sure I could sell that to the insurers. They're very bullish.'

Goode persisted. 'On a full valuation, quantum will be in excess of three hundred thousand pounds, and I don't think we can fail on liability. Must be worth a reasonable offer surely?'

'I'll see what they say, but my advice will be, at best, nuisance value. Are we allocated yet?'

'Yes,' Goode smiled serenely. 'We've got Lord Grey.' Well might he smile; a confirmed pursuers' man, Simon Grey. Pearson had been banking on the minimum, an even playing field, but no luck today. His bleeper vibrated, the text informing him 'Insurers at door'. A huddle of dark-suited men greeted him as he emerged into the hall and he knew, simply from their confident bearing, that they were expecting victory. He reported Goode's approach, and was unsurprised when they firmly rejected the very idea of a compromise; the matter should go to Proof, the pursuer must be required to establish her case. He had to agree, even though he was apprehensive about the forthcoming appearance. The tannoy became audible, announcing: 'Before Lord Grey... Court Four... Wylie v Murdoch...' The announcer dropped his voice to a whisper before booming out, 'Agents... Aird and Palfrey WS.and Salomon and Company. Court Four.'

The pursuer had given her evidence. Throughout it she had remained seated in the witness box, wearing some kind of neck brace and, eccentrically, a grubby spinal corset on the outside of her polo-neck jersey. Occasionally she grimaced, letting out, while speaking, apparently involuntarily, little groans. Ever since the accident she had been in horrendous pain, she said. Pain like no other experienced by anyone anywhere, her back was agony, her spine was rigid, she had a permanent sensation of spiders running up and down both thighs, and they regularly became burning hot or icy cold, even to the touch.

Pearson began his cross-examination by persuading her to go over her multiplicity of ailments once more. Her complaints became, with his surprisingly sympathetic approach, even worse, and by the time she had finished she was describing herself as a hopeless cripple, incapable of any pain-free movement. In the face of such understanding from her supposed adversary, she relaxed completely, exposing the soft underbelly of her gross exaggeration. Suddenly, his manner altered as he changed tack, drawing her attention to three medical reports compiled by her doctors, all of which suggested that she should have recovered from the effects of her accident within three months of its occurrence. How were they to be explained?

The Vixen joined Pearson in the cafeteria. He was attempting to swallow, still with no saliva, a tuna sandwich. His mind was on Christmas, and the best place to get a large tree. They'd need a new barrel for it, as the old one was no longer stable. He'd have to make the time to paint the new one red. He found Miss Fox's strong perfume headache-inducing rather than seductive. Oblivious to his wish to be alone, she immediately began to talk about their case.

'The pursuer did herself no favours this morning. All that nonsense about the sensation of spiders clambering up her legs!'

'Yes,' he replied wearily, wishing that someone somewhere would beam Miss Fox up or, at least, bleep her. Being no student of body language, she persisted.

'Should be good this afternoon. I've completed the joint minute, by the way, and it's being typed as we speak, so there's no need for any tedious wage-loss evidence.'

'Excellent,' Pearson said, rising while finishing his coffee in order to extricate himself from her unwelcome company. 'See you at two o'clock, Rowena.'

The court rose, as usual, at four pm, business then being considered to be completed for the day. Lord Grey, dressed in his silk robes, informed them all that he could not sit until ten-thirty the next morning, as he had criminal matters to deal with before the Proof could resume. All the lawyers present bowed to the judge when he stood up, then he was escorted off the bench to his chambers by his macer. Goode quickly edged along the bar clutching a large pile of disordered papers. 'Nuisance value offer still on the table?' he enquired wistfully. Pearson shook his head.

'No. The insurers want her blood now.'

He lifted his own heavy pile and exited the windowless court room. As the oak double doors swung behind him he was approached by Mr Edwards, one of the representatives of the insurance company. The man wanted to engage in a post mortem of the day's proceedings and Pearson knew that it would be politic to do so, but he was tired and hungry and had only twenty minutes in which to refuel before his next meeting. Consequently, he gestured silently at his watch and resumed his hurried walk away from Court Four. Having removed his wig and gown he went to the library to collect the next set of folders, his heart heavy in the knowledge that he would have to spend the evening working in the library. He silently ranted about Mrs Wylie. Thanks to her desire for ill-deserved compensation he'd have to forfeit the next three evenings at home, be deprived of doing any leisurely Christmas shopping and miss his youngest grandchild's first nativity play, in which she was to appear as a king. In the nearby tea-room, the 'Lower Aisle', he grabbed an egg roll, ate it quickly and with relish and then downed a hurried cup of tea.

His consultation with Dr McCrone went well. The eminent plastic surgeon had undertaken a bilateral mastectomy with breast reconstruction on a patient suffering from fibrocystic breast disease. He was accused of carrying out the operation without informing her of the possibility of a poor cosmetic outcome and the probability of impaired breast sensation. Fortunately, the aged consultant was able to point to abbreviations in the record of his pre-operative meeting with his patient which, he explained, represented his checklist for risks brought to the patient's attention. Opposite each abbreviation, including those standing for 'appearance' and 'sensation' were clear red tick marks.

David Pearson was relieved. The doctor had retired with an unblemished record, and the prospect of his reputation being tarnished at this late stage now seemed fairly remote. Nonetheless, the old fellow looked worried, and there was a patina of sweat on his brow which occasionally he wiped away with his handkerchief. He explained that he could remember the pursuer, Katrina Blackwell, perfectly well. She'd been experiencing, as she'd tearfully confided in him at their meeting, marital problems, and believed that her enhanced appearance might resolve her husband's sexual difficulties. In consequence of her high expectations he'd been at particular pains to emphasise the risks involved in the procedure itself and the spectrum of cosmetic and sensory outcomes that might follow it. He examined, as he spoke, the black and white photographs of the pursuer's left breast showing the rigid wrinkles and loose skin folds which disfigured it. His matter-of-fact manner left David Pearson unprepared for the images of bruised and distorted flesh passed to him, and he struggled not to grimace before returning the photos to the surgeon.

'I wish it had worked out better for the young lady,' Dr McCrone sighed. 'I did my best. No one seems to doubt that, luckily, but sometimes capsular contraction occurs and she was one of the unlucky ones. She's had two further operations you know, with Dr Small, both privately. One was for the removal of the… eh… submuscular implants and the insertion of subcutaneous ones and the other, I think, involved… eh… the removal of the subcutaneous ones, and substitution with anatomical implants. I haven't seen any photos but I gather she's quite happy with the… eh… end result.'

'Very good, doctor. Have we a date for the proof, yet?' the QC asked his solicitor.

She consulted her file. 'October, next year. It's been set down for ten days.'

'Excellent,' Pearson replied, gathering his papers to signal the end of the consultation.

'I am afraid there may be a problem, then,' Dr McCrone interjected. 'I have cancer, you know, and I might not be around.'

Without missing a beat, the two lawyers said together, 'Evidence on commission', and grinned at each other in recognition of their simultaneous answer to the problem, now solved.

David Pearson climbed the stairs from the lower consulting rooms and headed, without enthusiasm, to the waiting room. He saw Rose Ford, his next instructing agent, standing with her back to the gas fire. Their eyes met and he waved. She was such an attractive woman and highly intelligent with it. He was surer than ever that she fancied him. Hallelujah! No vacancy at present, but sooner or later one would come up, they always did. She crossed the room to greet him and broke her good news. The consultant neurosurgeon that they were due to meet had been unavoidably detained; he would be unable to attend and the consultation would have to be rescheduled for another day. Neither openly expressed their elation at this gift of time returned, but they left the consulting rooms together, each aware of the other's reaction.

By seven-thirty pm Pearson was the only soul left in the Advocates' Library. He was meticulously working his way through the copy of Mrs Wylie's general practice notes again. Her doctor was due to give evidence the next day, and the Silk had noted references to increasingly painful arthritis in the right wrist starting at about the time of the accident for which his clients were blamed. If the GP could be persuaded to speak to the disabling effect of the arthritic wrist, then he might be able to argue that whether or not they'd damaged her back she would, in any event, have been unable to continue to work due to her unrelated wrist condition. The doctor's writing was impossible and the photocopy was blurred. Abbreviations everywhere. He painstakingly marked, with a pink highlighter pen, all the entries of wrist complaints he could find in the copy records for easy reference in the court the next day. Having done this, he stretched, gathered his papers and dumped the whole lot in his box, to be forgotten about until the morning. If he could just get home quickly enough he might catch the tail-end of his favourite cookery programme, not that he ever cooked or intended to cook. But the cook herself, she was the draw.

He put on his overcoat and found his bicycle where he had left it propped up against the pillar. Bloody puncture! He scanned the frame for a pump, but the old model had long ago lost its original equipment and he'd never got round to replacing it. Pushing the bike by the handlebars, he began to walk to Merchiston Place. By the time he reached Forrest Road, torrential rain was falling, forming small brown rivers in the gutters and drenching the few unfortunates unable to take shelter. He hunched his shoulders and set off resolutely towards the Meadows.

7

The office cleaner left at ten pm and Alice breathed a sigh of relief. No more intrusive questions about her love life to be deflected, as if her nightly presence in the office until the woman's shift had ended was not sufficiently eloquent evidence of her unattached, unloved status. And, yes, she was aware of the ticking of her biological clock and yes, she did want kiddies but, she wanted to shout, being a little bit particular about the genetic make-up of my non-existent children, I can't just rush out to the nearest bar and get myself laid. Finding a suitable man is not easy, even if the alarm's gone off.

Feeling unsettled and humiliated, she collected her coat and began to search for her bag. The phone rang as she was doing so, and she knew immediately, instinctively, that it would be to tell her that the killer had struck again. Sure enough, Inspector Manson broke the news. The body was in the Meadows.

The car journey there took Alice less than ten minutes, despite the downpour soaking the city. She left the dry warmth of her vehicle reluctantly, setting off on foot for the large public park. When, for the second time, the wind tried to force her umbrella out of her hands, she pulled it closer to herself, aware that it afforded little protection from rain that changed direction with every gust, but reluctant to abandon its shelter altogether. Another strong blast and it had been turned inside out, the fabric flapping noisily from exposed spines, leaving huge raindrops to fall, freely, onto her head. Exasperated, she flung it down and began to run, turning right down Jawbone Walk, drawn to the arc lights and striped tape that delineated the boundaries of the scene. She could feel cold water streaming down her face and neck, dripping from her hands, splashing her unprotected legs, chilling her to the bone.

Uniformed officers, moving slowly in the bitter wind, were trying to erect a screen around the corpse, simply to shield it from the curious eyes and intrusive cameras of the press. She reached the body and looked down at it, conscious that she was panting loudly and that water was cascading off her raincoat, mingling with the pool of blood surrounding the prostrate figure and sending up little pink splashes with each drop. The man was lying spreadeagled on the ground, face and throat uppermost, revealing a hideous, crescent-shaped gash that ran from ear to ear like an extra, gaping mouth. Dark blood had pooled in an eye socket, making a huge black orb. The uncovered body was soaked and a strand of hair moved continually, caught in one of the rivulets created by the downpour. No one had been assigned to arrange shelter for the corpse, so Alice took the task on, knowing that she would be unable to concentrate properly until it was completed, not that his flesh could feel anything now. He had been robbed of his life and all dignity; a dead dog in a gutter would have had more.

While she was preoccupied, fretting about the victim's vulnerability to the elements, she busied herself attempting to reattach a sheet of awning to the makeshift screen it had freed itself from. DC Ruth Littlewood came to assist, and together they managed to subdue the billowing canvas and tether it to the frame, finally creating some kind of temporary refuge from the weather for themselves and the body at their feet. Ruth wiped the rainwater from her eyes with a tissue, and then passed an opaque little polythene bag, sealed at the neck, to her superior.

'Another note?' Alice asked, knowing the answer already.

'Yup. Found it in the bloke's left hand pocket. Blue biro this time, and the word's "misleading". It's on stiff paper, more like card or something.'

'Who found the body?'

'A girl, a student at the University. She's called Jane Drummond. I'll go and get her for you shall I?'

'Where is she now?'

'Sheltering by the pavilion. DC Porter's with her.'

'I'll go there. The photographers will need this space soon and the presence of the body won't help the witnesses' concentration.'

Under the eaves of the boarded-up pavilion a girl was standing, shivering with cold, trying unsuccessfully to light a cigarette despite the wind and lashing rain. She looked up on Alice's approach and started to return the damp cigarette to its packet, but her hand was shaking violently, making the manoeuvre unusually difficult. Tears were falling down her already wet face.

'Jane, there are just a few matters I need to talk to you about, can you manage?' Alice enquired.

'Yes,' the girl answered in a whisper.

'I've been told that you were coming from the Meadow Place side of the park and heading towards the old Royal Infirmary when you came across the body, is that right?'

'Yes,' another faint reply.

'Can you tell me when that was?'

The student sniffed, cleaning her eyes with her fists like a small child, before composing herself and answering in a near-normal voice, 'I think it would've been at about a quarter past nine. I looked at my watch when I was waiting for the ambulance, the police, and it was about twenty past then. I found him and phoned almost immediately.'

'When you found him, was he already dead?'

'As far as I could tell, yes,' she gulped, 'not moving, with that huge slash on his throat. He didn't say anything, his eyes were shut, blood everywhere. I didn't take his pulse, if that's what you mean. Should I have?'

'No, no, don't worry,' Alice reassured her. 'There was nothing you could have done. Truly. Before you found him, did you see anyone else in the area?'

'No. I had my head down because of the rain. I wanted to get back to the flat as quickly as possible. I only saw the poor guy because I practically tripped over his bike. It was lying right across my path and there he was, right next to it. If I'd been a few feet further to the left or right I would have missed him completely.'

'When you were phoning or waiting with the body did you see anyone?'

The girl hesitated, before responding, 'I think there was a cyclist... Sorry not to be sure, but I got such a shock... It's difficult to recall... I just keep seeing that awful cut...'

'A cyclist?'

'Yes, going across the grass on the right-hand side... A good distance from me, though. I couldn't even say if it was a man or a woman. Whoever it was had their head down and their bum high off the saddle, like, trying to get out of the wet.'

'Anyone else?'

'No, I don't think so.'

'Certain?'

'Certain as I can be, but I wasn't looking. I was just standing by that poor man, praying for the ambulance, the police, anyone to come and help. His head was practically off...' The sentence remained unfinished, as the witness suddenly covered her mouth with her hand, before doubling up and vomiting copiously onto the tarmac at her feet.

Alice left the pavilion and returned to the body of David Pearson. In the little crowd assembling behind the boundary tape, she recognised a couple of unwelcome faces, James Mitchell from the *Scotsman*, unmissable as ever in his black fedora hat, and the red-lipsticked giantess from the *Evening*

News. Wherever blood had been spilt they were to be found, like sharks, honed by evolution for their unsavoury task, single-minded and transfixed by the newest death. Mitchell, spying her, tipped the brim of his hat and she managed to smile at him. In the past he had helped her, and maybe would again. No point in alienating an ally, particularly a ruthless predator like him.

Manson, raincoat flapping open and belt whipping his sides, approached the giantess. Another of the strange symbiotic relationships created as a result of a murder, she thought. Sheltering beneath the policeman's umbrella, the journalist appeared rapt by whatever information she was receiving, apparently memorising everything, notebook closed in her hand. Manson would, no doubt, be favouring her with his drugs theory, imparted earlier to Alice on the phone and as quickly dismissed by her. Dr Clarke, a medical practitioner, would have access to drugs and might have gone 'rotten'; Sammy McBryde could hardly have lived where he did and not been a user, possibly even a dealer; and Pearson, a Queen's Counsel, would know half of the drugs barons in central Scotland, no doubt having saved their poxy skins and earned their undying gratitude.

Thursday 8th December

The squad meeting, held at nine am precisely, was packed. Detective Superintendent Brunson was seated beside DCI Bell and Charlie Whyte, the press officer from HQ at Fettes, was standing, coffee cup in hand, by the door. As soon as DCI Bell rose the chatter in the room ceased, replaced by an attentive silence, as all eyes focused upon her. Her voice was still husky, unnaturally low, and any address would have to be given without frills or she'd be reduced to a whispering wreck again.

'All of you will be aware, by now, that our killer has struck again. Identical M.O., knife or whatever across the throat, and another little piece of paper. The word this time is "misleading", and it was found in one of the victim's trouser pockets, the left one. Different paper, unlined, and different ink, blue on this occasion. The locus of the killing was the Meadows. The victim, David Pearson QC, was crossing them some time between about eight-forty-five pm and nine-fifteen pm. We know he left the Faculty of Advocates in the High Street at eight-forty-five pm as he clocked out then and filled in their register. He was found dead by a witness, Jane Drummond, some time around nine-fifteen pm. Uniforms are already doing further door-to-doors around Bankes Crescent, Learmonth Terrace and the Medway, and we've added all addresses about the Meadows onto their list. The post mortem on Pearson is at twelve today and I want Alastair and Alice to attend. I need Sandy and Ruth to oversee the search of the Meadows and its surroundings and DCs Irwin and Sinclair can assist the Dog Section.'

A muffled 'woof, woof' could be heard from Colin Irwin and Graham Sinclair's direction, followed by a spontaneous chorus of 'Who Let the Dogs Out', *sotto voce* and inaudible to Elaine Bell. Unaware of the squad's antics she continued: 'This type of attack, throat-cutting with a sharp instrument…'. She stopped in mid-sentence as Laurence Body, Assistant Chief Constable, entered the room. He acknowledged his Chief Inspector and took a seat at the back beside a group of individuals that had not formed part of the squad before. Bell picked up her thread and persevered, '…as I was saying, this type of attack, throat-cutting with a sharp knife, is not common. There are two men in Barlinnie who favoured such a method of killing and a couple of loons in Carstairs but, so far, we haven't found anyone out and about who's known to wield knives, or whatever, in this way. All the mental hospitals are being checked and I'd like DCs MacDonald and Lindsay to go this morning to Stratheden to enquire into a possible candidate. The manager's expecting a visit. They've got all the records there and the pair of you can get details of what precisely we're looking for from Sandy. He's just been accessing Holmes…' DS Sandy Moray gave a thumbs up sign to no-one in particular.

Alice's attention had begun to drift away from the meeting. She was vaguely aware of the DCI introducing the new members of the squad—presumably the individuals seated beside ACC Body—just a list of names, Travers, Carter, Cockburn, going on and on. In her mind she had already reached the mortuary and was standing outside a white door, waiting to go in, steeling herself for the awful sights she expected to see, the awful scents she expected to smell. The clicking of Alastair's fingers before her eyes returned her to reality, the interruption softened by a proffered cup of tea.

'What did you think of Manson's little surprise on Thursday?' he enquired, sipping his coffee.

'Ian Melville's fingerprints in Dr Clarke's flat?' she replied.

'Yes.'

'Well… I suppose it tells us as a minimum that Melville wasn't telling us the truth and that Mansons don't change their spots? If Melville was involved in Dr Clarke's death, he must have had an accomplice.'

'Yeh,' he agreed, 'the two identical sets in Bankes Crescent and Granton would have to be those of his accomplice, eh? Melville might or might not have been present in McBryde's place. He could have been careful in Granton but have slipped up in Dr Clarke's flat.'

'Mmm, that's what I thought too. We'll need to check on that woman who answered his phone, too. Have you seen Roddy Cohen yet?'

'No, the sod had gone out. I never got a chance to speak to him. I'm going to try again today.'

David Pearson lay on the trolley, naked, exposed to the gaze of all, waiting to be manhandled onto the table. Alice was astonished by his hairiness; he was like a chimpanzee, and an instant image of him wearing a party hat and sipping tea with other chimps flashed into her mind. Appalled by the picture she had involuntarily created, she dragged her thoughts away from the tea-party scene and back to the immobile, hirsute form now on the table. The surreal sound of bodily fluids being tapped became audible and she looked away from the body, resting her eyes on a collection of silvery scalpels arranged by size in a basin. Aware of a strange organic smell, she fought against the impulse to clamp her hand over her nose and mouth and concentrated instead on counting the metallic tools in the dish. The odour was becoming overpowering, and the hum of the saw, buzzing angrily, changed as it made contact with the scalp. A strange popping sound accompanied the removal of the top of the cranium, like the noise when a cork is extracted from a bottle. It's just a film, she thought, not reality. I could walk out at any minute, I don't have to stay if I don't want to.

Her strategy for coping was destroyed by the sound of an irate voice close to her ear, 'Sit down, Sergeant. There's a chair over there.' Thinking the remark had been addressed to her, she began to move away from the table, only to hear a thud as Alastair seated himself at the pathologist's desk. He had his head in his hands, elbows on his knees, and was retching dryly into a bowl held by an assistant, also clad in green scrubs. Some time soon, please God, their ordeal would be over, everything weighed, measured, bagged and labelled, and the desecrated body returned to the fridge. Feeling slightly faint, she inadvertently caught the eye of the principal pathologist, and he winked at her through his half-moon spectacles. Noticing tiny spots of yellow fluid on his lenses, her legs gave way beneath her and she slumped, senseless, to the floor.

Friday 9th December

No birdsong in the winter, just the sound of the traffic starting up in the city, gears being changed, exhaust fumes being pumped out. Seven am and the din made by the alarm by her bed was augmented by the unwelcome tones of the telephone. She turned over and fumbled for the receiver.

'Alice?' It was Inspector Manson's voice.

'Yes, Sir,' she responded thickly, as if unused to speech.

'Can you meet me in the station in half an hour?'

'Of course, Sir.' Pointless to enquire why; Alice knew she would not be wanted if anyone else was available. By the time she reached St Leonard's, ten minutes late, the Inspector was sitting in Alastair's chair with his feet up, reading a copy of Ian Melville's statement. He folded it as she entered the room, collected his jacket and did a revolving gesture with his fingers to tell her to retrace her steps and leave the building. On the way to see Melville, or 'the perpetrator' as the Detective Inspector had taken to calling him, Manson explained that he would handle the interview in its entirety; she should take no part in it due to its sensitivity. Alice was not sure whether this observation was intended to provoke, or whether the man truly believed that only his discriminating handling would be appropriate. Let it pass.

One parking space was available in the Colonies, so they took it, and walked back across the Water of Leith to St Bernard's Row. Ian Melville was up and dressed, and answered the knock on his front door himself. Alice scrutinised his face as he took in her presence. No sign of fear or even anxiety, although he had lied to her and was intelligent enough to know that this follow-up visit was probably attributable to his deception. As Inspector Manson began to enter the flat, Melville politely requested the policeman to put out his cigar. Manson gave one last, exaggerated draw and then dropped his Havana onto the sanded boards, grinding it under his heel messily, and all the while staring into Melville's eyes. Flashing his identity card, he walked into the kitchen and, uninvited, sat in one of the wooden chairs flanking the table. He was like a terrier, excited, eager to break the back of the rat. No need for any preliminaries, best clamp the jaws round the rodent's spine, shake, and quickly dispatch.

'You lied, Mr Melville. Not a wise thing to do.'

'In what respect, Inspector?' Melville did not appear perturbed by the accusation.

'Your prints... They were all over Dr Clarke's flat.' A clear exaggeration, and Alice crossed her arms and leant back in her chair, unconsciously distancing herself from her superior.

'I was Dr Clarke's boyfriend for quite a long period. I tended not to wear rubber gloves all the time.' Melville's emerging disdain for his interrogator was unmistakable.

'These prints... on a glass... are recent. Dr Clarke had a cleaner. She washed her employer's used crockery, and glasses, every day, first thing.' Manson spoke slowly, enunciating each word, apparently savouring the killer blow as he landed it, not bothering to hide the smile of triumph that had crept over his face.

'I didn't tell the sergeants the whole truth,' Melville said, glancing at Alice apologetically. 'I did see Elizabeth on Thursday night. I went to her flat after I left my studio. I wanted to find out if we could be friends. I thought maybe if she'd let me be a friend again, then we'd have a chance of getting back together. I've never made any bones about the fact that I loved her, to you. She allowed me in, and that was an improvement, as she'd slammed the door the last time I went to her house. I brought her flowers, freesias, I think. I just wanted to see her, to talk to her, to be in the same room, but she didn't want anything to do with me, really. She gave me a glass of wine, but never poured out one for herself, so I knew I wouldn't be there long. She was polite, she kept apologising, saying that she had an important medico-legal report to prepare, but I reckoned that she simply didn't like having me anywhere near her. She wouldn't look me in the face, or meet my eyes, kept looking into space, and the only time our eyes did meet, she flinched. If you know somebody well they don't have to say much for the message to get across...'

'And then what?' Manson interrupted.

'And then nothing,' Melville replied coldly. 'I left. End of story.'

'You expect me to believe that!' Manson expostulated.

'No. Precisely because I did not expect your kind to believe "that" I omitted "that" and my expectation has not been exceeded. A woman is murdered, one I loved. The woman who killed my child and I fell out with. The woman seen by me on the night of the killing. Ergo, plod, I done it. I knew that's how it would seem to you, and lo and behold, that's how it does seem to you.'

'I think,' the Inspector leant over the table in his eagerness to express his theory, 'that you went to Dr Clarke's flat, you were determined to re-establish your relationship with her, and when she refused, you lost it, you killed her…'

'You didn't need to tell me that, I knew that's what you'd think. But we live in different worlds, Inspector. Yours drips with blood wherever you look. Mine's different. In mine, people in love don't kill each other. I have loved before, you know, I have lost before, you know. No, I haven't had my unborn child killed before, but I know Liz saw things quite differently, she's a gynaecologist, for Christ's sake. She had performed countless abortions. I loved her and so I forgave her. Once she'd loved me, then she didn't. It happens, it made me sad, not mad. I wish she was still alive, I wish I'd never seen her that night, I wish I had an alibi, but I don't, and that doesn't make me her killer, whatever you may think.'

Undaunted by Melville's impassioned speech, the terrier clumsily attempted to corner his prey again.

'We know you take drugs, no point in denying it. Did Dr Clarke supply you with them?'

Melville was unable, or unwilling, to conceal his contempt any longer, and shook his head with disbelief before answering.

'As I said, we live in different worlds, on different planets, in different bloody universes. In my twenties, like nearly everyone else I knew, I took drugs. Since then I've taken nothing, so I have no idea, I repeat NO IDEA, where you got your inaccurate, half-baked information. The idea of Elizabeth supplying them…', he laughed mirthlessly, '…is so preposterous as not to deserve an answer. Her entire career was devoted to improving people's health. Why not go the whole hog and accuse your own Chief Constable of peddling? He'd be as likely, actually, quite possibly more likely. If these are the sorts of flights of fancy you engage in for the purposes of your investigation, Inspector, Elizabeth's murderer will be at large for ever, laughing at you as you reach out for the next red herring or wild goose. Maybe you should try and keep your big feet on the ground, stick to the facts…'

'We don't need any instruction in detection from you, Melville, and you'd better tell the truth, the whole truth and nothing but the truth from now on. I've met your smart-arse type before…'

Disobeying the express command she had been given earlier, Alice broke into the duel between the two men. 'The woman who answered your phone on Tuesday, who was she?'

'Must have been Paula.' Evidently all co-operation had now been withdrawn, even monosyllables would have to be teased out.

'Paula, who?' she persisted.

'Paula Carruthers.'

'And your relationship with her?'

'Occasional sleeping partner.' Melville had chosen his words carefully.

'Not a girlfriend then?'

He smiled wearily before answering, 'No. For me there's a difference. You asked me, last time, about girlfriends, and I said I'd had none since Liz. I was telling you the truth, although you may think I'm lying. Liz and I were lovers and friends, we didn't just have sex with each other. Since we broke up I have slept with other women, but I haven't loved any of them, had any kind of lasting relationship with them or even wanted to. Paula's no different. The answer I gave you originally was completely accurate by my lights. Anything else?'

As Inspector Manson said 'No', Alice said, 'Yes. Can you tell me what time it was when you left Elizabeth Clarke's flat?'

'About eight o'clock,' he replied.

Alastair had left the draft post mortem report on David Pearson up on the computer screen and Alice glanced at it:

> 'External examination—the body was that of a middle-aged white male, measuring approximately six foot one inch in height and weighing approximately eighty kg. The head hair was dark brown, streaked with grey, of moderate length and straight. The eyes were brown. There were no petechial haemorrhages, there was no jaundice. The mouth contained natural dentition in a reasonable state in both the upper and lower jaws. There was no evidence of injury within the mouth...'

She flicked, idly, to the post mortem reports for Elizabeth Clarke and Sammy McBryde, all equally impersonal, couched in the same clinical language; cold, objective, as if describing a cut of meat. Like a painting by Lucien Freud, accurate to the nth degree, but shocking, as if executed by a member of another species, an alien intelligence incapable of perceiving anything beyond the flesh and bones.

'Imagining your own post mortem report?' Alastair broke his companion's concentration..

'It will state,' she replied airily, 'the body was that of a woman in her prime, measuring approximately six foot in height and of appropriate weight for a wonderfully slim build. The head hair was a dark, glossy chestnut, curled luxuriantly and naturally. The eyes were of hazel surrounded by thick, upturned lashes… the full lips contained regular, pearly white teeth…'

'Internal examination', Alastair interrupted '…the soul, on close inspection, was found to be completely black.' The phone rang. It was DCI Elaine Bell, croaky as ever and crunching in between sentences another cough sweet. Montgomery, in his caravan at El Alamein, could not have pushed himself harder than the ill little policewoman. They were to go, first thing the next day, to speak to Pearson's widow. Kid gloves were to be worn and no feathers ruffled as the ACC (Crime) knew her family and was positively chummy with her mother. The press had already been making nuisances of themselves, staking out the place, and if they were still present, as seemed likely, they were to be provided with no titbits whatsoever, however innocuous they might seem. The words 'serial killer' had already appeared in an article in one of the tabloid papers, even though nothing had been officially provided by anyone from Fettes HQ suggesting that such a creature was at large. Manson's report on the Ian Melville interview was now on Holmes, and the suspect already under surveillance.

8

Saturday 10th December

Judging by his house, David Pearson QC had been a successful advocate. The large, three-storied sandstone building dwarfed its respectable neighbours, trumpeting the prosperity of its owner, his dominance of Merchiston Crescent. A pair of wide herbaceous borders flanked the paved path that led to the front door, every shrub in them neatly cut back, every seed head topped, a garden in which order and control were the watchwords, nature required to be subdued rather than indulged.

As Alice fumbled ineffectually beneath an over-sized, prickly Christmas wreath for the door knocker, Alastair yanked the brass bell-pull. A cleaner, who appeared to have the ability to disappear at will, showed them into the living room. On a regency striped sofa two women were seated. The elder of the pair was cradling the hand of her companion in her own but she dropped it on becoming aware of the presence of strangers, sitting up straight and crossing her arms defensively on her breast. She was tall and slim, gaunt almost, and once must have been beautiful, but age had eaten away at her looks, leaving her impressive rather than attractive, more interesting than appealing. One thing was unmistakable about her, though, the strength of her character; and her heavy-lidded gaze seemed to challenge whomsoever's it met. The woman by her side, dressed faux-casually in a cream linen suit, rose to receive the intruders.

'Hello. I'm Laura Pearson.' She stretched out her hand in greeting and then introduced them to the woman beside her, her mother, Mrs Winter. The old lady remained seated, but acknowledged the police presence by the slightest incline of her head. Alice, beginning to take in her surroundings, was again struck by the irreconcilability of things; of this cosy, domestic, scene with the mud, blood and rain in the Meadows; of the silver-framed photos of a smiling, be-suited man in a white tie, wig and gown and the grey, hairy corpse splayed out on the mortuary table with the crown of the skull removed, like the top of a boiled egg. Somehow information must be extracted without causing further pain and upset, an impossible task even when time had allowed the wounds to heal. Aware that a start had to be made somewhere, Alice launched in.

'We need information on a number of matters, Mrs Pearson. I'm sorry to have to trouble you with questions so soon after your husband's death, but it's necessary in order to track down his killer.'

'I quite understand,' the widow replied.

'First of all, can you tell me when you were expecting your husband back, on the night of the murder?'

Laura Pearson sighed. 'Whenever he arrived, really. It's the nature of the job. I knew his proof was due to start, and that if it couldn't be settled he'd have to work late. That's the normal pattern. If he manages to settle his case in the morning then he almost always comes home and returns to the Faculty later for any consultations, if any have been arranged. You see, they can't start until after four pm, when the proof's over for the day, so there's a reasonable gap before he has to return. Anyway, as he didn't come back before lunch I knew that the proof must be running and that he'd be staying on late at the Faculty. He'd talked quite a bit about it, and I knew that there were lots of papers and some difficult medical stuff. This time he was quite worked up about it all. He's always a bit tense when there's a lot of material to take in, and he said that he thought his opponent would be unhelpful to boot. So I didn't know when he'd be back exactly. Just sometime in the evening and probably, if he could make it, before a particular programme on TV that he liked. We have a sort of system. I always have some cold things in the fridge so that we're not caught out, and I eat alone if he's not back by about seven pm.'

'And you were in that evening, by yourself?'

'Yes. I was finishing off the Christmas cards.' She stopped, and then continued, musing to herself, 'I don't know why he was walking across the Meadows.'

'How did you expect him to come home?'

'By bike, as he usually did.'

'What sort of practice did your husband have?' Alice continued.

'Why do you ask?' She looked anxious, unsure of the relevance of the question, as if it might have been almost impertinent.

'Well, was he a civil lawyer or did he do crime or what?'

'He'd been purely civil for years. His speciality was medical negligence, usually for the defenders, the hospital doctors. Sometimes he did pursuers' work too, but that tended to be Legal Aid, so he only did it when he absolutely had to, as it's so poorly paid.'

'Can you think of anyone that might have had enough of a grievance against your husband to kill him?'

The directness of her own question appalled Alice.

'No, I can't think of anyone,' came back the reply. The widow, at least, appeared to have taken the question in her stride. Alice saw, out of the corner of her eye, Alastair mouth the word 'oaf', and while she was thinking how to formulate her next question Mrs Winter broke in.

'David's killer was, probably, some kind of madman. I expect that my son-in-law just happened to cross the wrong path at the wrong time or some such thing. I doubt very much that his murderer knew him or anything about him. Consequently, the question of a motive very probably won't arise.' The statement was accompanied by a hostile stare directed at Alice.

Alastair, seeing that his partner had stalled, took up the questioning.

'Mrs Pearson, do you know anyone called Samuel McBryde?'

'No.' The answer was immediate, unhesitating.

'What about your husband, did he know the man?'

'I don't think that he knew anyone of that name. If he did I certainly never heard him mention it. He could have known... Mr McBryde... in a work context, I suppose. All I can say is that I'm not aware of him knowing any such person.'

'What about Dr Elizabeth Clarke, did your husband know her?'

'No! No, no. I don't...'

As she spoke, Laura Pearson shook her head repeatedly. She continued to meet her interrogator's gaze, but tears had begun to flow uncontrollably from her large brown eyes. She appeared to have no hanky, and made no attempt to dab her eyes or staunch the now unstoppable stream.

'Just carry on,' she said, 'ignore these... I cry far too easily. It doesn't mean I can't answer your questions quite sensibly. Please take no notice.'

But before either of the sergeants could continue, Mrs Winter whisked a hanky from her sleeve, handed it to her daughter and took over.

'Constables, I think this discussion must come to a close now. My daughter has done her best to answer your questions at what is, evidently, a very difficult time for her. She needs to rest. She didn't sleep last night, and the doctor's due to come here shortly. I'm afraid we really must ask you to go.' In reality there was no 'we' about it, and it was not a request.

'There are just a few additional things we need to know,' Alice persisted. 'In particular, a bit about Mr Pearson's background, friends, or...'

'No.' Mrs Winter's voice, interrupting the unfinished question, brooked no resistance. To clinch the matter she stood up, standing protectively in front of her still-seated daughter, and gestured with her hand towards the living room door. The two sergeants moved obediently towards it, but as they were doing so Laura Pearson said, 'You could speak to Alan…'

'Alan who?'

'Alan Duncan, QC. He was David's best friend, both before and after they were called to the Bar. He lives in Ann Street.'

Blood in the water. The sharks were circling the Pearsons' exit, waiting for a titbit of flesh, alert and active but not yet frenzied. Alice caught sight of the red-lipped giantess at the back, jostling with the rest of them, elbows raised, craning for a view of any of the members of the 'grieving family' as they emerged. The buzz of excitement died down as soon as the press realised that none of the dead man's relatives were leaving the house, and on being met with the Detective Sergeants' 'No comment' to their every shouted enquiry.

Ann Street is, as is well known within the New Town, the apotheosis of social arrival: no-one lives there who has not made it or inherited it. If a bomb were to explode in the centre of the narrow precinct, the corridors of power would become unaturally silent and the New Club's income would be halved at a blow. Not a single satellite dish disfigures its elegant architecture, and the presence of one would be as unlikely, and unwelcome, as a catamite in a convent.

Alan Duncan QC was expecting his visitors. In his stockinged feet he led his two guests through his house and into a warm study at the back of the building. Hardly an inch of carpet was visible in it; the entire floor surface was covered in mounds of paper, all radiating outwards from the centre of the room where there was a table and three chairs. With ease the large man navigated through the tottering piles to reach his own seat and indicated for the two sergeants to follow him. Like a couple of Wenceslas's pages they tiptoed nervously, stepping onto his exact footsteps, aware that a wrong move, a careless step, could result in an avalanche of papers. Duncan picked up a pen and twiddled it between his fat, pink fingers, and Alice, watching, was struck that he bore more resemblance to a stout Stirlingshire farmer, with his ruddy complexion, soup plates for hands and brawny forearms, than any kind of pen-pusher. No boneless white fingers or flaccid, wasted muscles on him, so characteristic of a life spent in libraries or courtrooms, breathing re-circulated air and drinking too much coffee.

'Can you tell us a bit about David Pearson? When did you first meet?' Alastair enquired.

'We met at university, at Edinburgh. In our second year we shared a flat together in Morningside, that's how he got to know, and love, that side of the city. After graduating, he thought he'd make lots of money, so he joined the Commercial Department of Dundas & Stirling WS and I got a Bar apprenticeship with Rattrays. Eventually, he decided that corporate work wasn't for him and he joined me up at the Faculty. We've been friends since we were about eighteen and I shall miss him dearly.' The lawyer's intonation was clipped, the vowels old-fashioned, like a cruel parody of a broadcast to the Empire by a pre-war monarch.

'What sort of work did he do at the Bar, any crime?'

'None at all.' He corrected himself before continuing, 'Well, virtually none. He was forced for a bit to be an ad hoc advocate depute, you know, a temporary prosecutor, but he hated it and avoided as many circuits as he could. He probably only prosecuted about eight cases, if that, during the entire stint. All fairly small beer anyway. They only give the lesser stuff to the ad hocs. I doubt if his demise is associated with any prosecution work carried out by him, and he never did any criminal defence work. His speciality, as Laura probably told you, was medical negligence defence work. He could make a good living out of it and it genuinely interested him. He used to marvel, after some consultation with, say, a colorectal surgeon or whatever, that he'd get paid, effectively, for a lesson in a subject which he so enjoyed. Sometimes agents used to try and get him involved in commercial work, but any interest he'd ever had in such stuff had long since palled, so he'd sidestep it if he could.'

'He was doing well?'

'He was doing very well. Financially, at least. He had more work than he needed and he could pick and choose his cases as a result. He wasn't really a Faculty man, none of your Bench and Bar golf or that kind of thing, and he wasn't remotely interested in any of the Faculty offices, Dean, Treasurer or whatever.'

'Would he have made it onto the Bench, been appointed a judge?'

'I doubt that. Too human, untidy, undisciplined and uninterested.'

'What do you mean, "too human"?'

'David was rather over-fond of women for a married man. Too fond for his own good or Laura's. He strayed numerous times both before and after Laura. Strayed with that Clarke woman for a start.'

Neither sergeant batted an eyelid.

'That Clarke woman?' Alastair enquired.

'You know, Dr Elizabeth Clarke, the woman who was murdered last week. They got to know each other through work and the knowledge became biblical. She was used as an expert in some case or other of his and, as usual, he toppled off his pedestal and onto her attractive lap. It wasn't just a fling, this time. It must have lasted at least six months. A full-blooded affair.'

'Did his wife know about it?'

'She could hardly have failed to do so in the circumstances.

David and Elizabeth were returning together in a car from some jolly or other, probably at Greywalls or some other smart hotel, when they had a road traffic accident. I can't remember which of them was driving. As they were going through Macmerry, or maybe Pencaitland, they ran over a little boy. The police were called and it was all over the *East Lothian Courier*, the *Scotsman*, the usual papers. Thankfully, nothing came of it, as whoever was driving wasn't considered to be at fault. But it was, in a small way, a *cause célèbre* amongst the chattering medico-legal classes, in fact a first-class scandal, well worth repeating in the New Town. Needless to say, Laura was completely humiliated, and no wonder, it was so public, but she accepted David back, yet again. More than he deserved, although he was, for all his faults, an extraordinarily likeable man, and her life with him was never dull. I think that's what he gave to Laura, excitement, sparkle. Fizz, if you will, but all at a high price.'

'When did all of this happen?'

'Oh, quite a long time ago. I should think... five, six years... certainly, before he was made a Silk.'

'Did he continue his relationship with Dr Clarke after the accident?'

'No. I'm pretty certain that he ended it then. As I say, Laura had become aware of it and I think he was faced with a stark choice between keeping his marriage alive or continuing with Elizabeth Clarke.'

'And, evidently, he chose his wife?'

'Yes, but for once it was finely balanced. I think he really loved Elizabeth Clarke and I suspect that if things hadn't ended in the way that they did, his marriage might well have died of natural causes and then he'd have married Elizabeth. No doubt he'd have led her a merry dance too. I'm not sure he was capable of being faithful.'

'Did he remain in contact with Dr Clarke at all?'

'Only on a professional basis, as far as I know. He told me

that he'd have to see her as she'd been chosen as the expert witness in some of the court actions in which he was involved. Counsel often don't get to choose their experts, otherwise she wouldn't have been. I do remember him talking, earlier this year, about some worrying case in which they were caught up. More recently, they were both speakers in some conference that David had organised about human rights and assisted reproduction.'

A lithe Siamese kitten peered round the door and slunk over to its master's chair, purring and twining its sinuous brown tail around his legs before being scooped up onto his lap. A massive forefinger stroked its fragile head and it closed its eyes in ecstasy, flexing its claws in and out with pleasure.

'Did his marriage recover, as far as you're aware?' Alistair's questioning continued.

'Yes. To its pre-Clarke state at least.'

'And what was that?'

'As I said, David was over-fond of women for a married man. So, if an opportunity arose he took it and if an opportunity could be made, he made it. His last Euro-devil…' Alastair intervened.

'His last what?'

'Euro-devil. It's a Law Society scheme. In essence, young high-flying lawyers from the European Union, and beyond, come to Scotland for some legal experience and for part of their time they are allocated to "shadow", if you will, a member or members of the Bar. "Devil" means "apprentice", really. David's last one was a rather attractive girl from Vilnius. I have little doubt that they spent as much time in the advocate's bedroom as they did in the Advocates' Library. He was incorrigible…' Duncan laughed. 'I heard a rumour in the gown room only the other day that he had made another conquest, a lady member, but I never had a chance to talk to him about it. I've been away for the last three weeks in the Black Isle, doing an agricultural arbitration at Munlochy. Too late now.'

'So judgeship, the Bench, wasn't likely due to his womanising?'

'No. The Bench wasn't likely due to his *untidy* womanising. It was the untidiness that was the problem.'

'Was Mrs Pearson aware what he was up to?'

'After Elizabeth, you mean?'

'Yes.'

'Probably not. Well, maybe at some deep level. I think for years she's wilfully blinded herself to what's going on. She couldn't change him or her affection for him. She was forced to face the Clarke affair, but after that, just as before that, she put the blinkers on herself. You see they did actually have a lot together, even if all passion had been spent. And then there were the children. Laura was a law student with David and me, she's probably more intelligent than either of us. My wife can't understand how she put up with David, but then Hilary never liked him and has always been unmoved by his charms. Fortunately for me.'

'The traffic accident you mentioned, in which a child died. You don't know who was at the wheel?'

'No. I suspect it was probably Elizabeth, as David actively disliked driving. He was strangely uncoordinated. He used a bike whenever he could although, God knows, he's had enough near misses to ground any sensible cyclist. He never drove a car unless he absolutely had to.'

'And the accident took place in Macmerry?'

'Macmerry or Pencaitland. Yes.'

'About five or six years ago?'

'Yes.'

Alan Duncan's wife appeared at the study door. In her arms was a huge cardboard box which was obviously heavy. She dropped it theatrically, making a tremendous thud and causing a little shiver of documents to fall from the surrounding piles.

'Message from the agents, darling. The arbitration at Munlochy's back on. It starts on Monday,' she said, looking at her husband as the kitten, startled by the noise, jumped from his lap.

'Blast!' He shook his head as if in disbelief, before turning his attention back to his visitors.

'I'm afraid I'm going to be busy with that stuff for the rest of the day. Three huge files of correspondence that I've never seen before and my time to do so is pretty limited. I'm sorry... I hope I've been able to help a bit. Let me know if there's anything else you need and I'll do my best to assist in any way that I can, but not any more today.'

The pool Astra was trapped. Cars had been parked at either end of it, leaving no more than a few inches between bonnet and bumper.

'Bugger!' Alastair shouted. Alice glanced at her friend, noticing for the first time how flushed he appeared, and that sweat had gathered beneath his eyes. The slight yellowing of facial skin that sometimes accompanies flu showed around his temples and cheeks, and she remembered, suddenly thinking it significant, that he had been coughing on and off throughout the interview with Alan Duncan. I'm doomed to flu now too, she thought, but said only: 'You okay?'

'No. I've caught something and I feel terrible. I'll have to go home. I never managed to see Cohen on Wednesday and I'm supposed to be seeing him today. Could you do it for me?'

'No trouble. I'll drop you off and then go on to him. We need to follow up Duncan's information about the Clarke-Pearson connection. It's gold dust, I reckon. The parents of the dead child could well want the pair of them dead.'

'Yeh,' her companion replied, without enthusiasm.

Alice inched forward, reversed, inched forward, reversed, until, at long last, the car was angled for an exit into the cobbled street. But as the pavements were lined with fat vehicles, SUVs, BMWs and Volvos, there was insufficient room for traffic to pass in both directions, and the cars in the centre were stationary due to a stand-off between two obstinate residents. Finally, one gave way and began to reverse, and Alice was allowed, with much smiling and waving, into the slow stream of northbound traffic.

Roderick Cohen was delighted by the unexpected female company, and the fact that the visit was official as opposed to social did not appear to register or, if it did, it did not diminish his ill-concealed joy. Alice examined the armchair that it appeared she was supposed to share with a moulting white rabbit, shooed the creature away and sat down carefully, as if an inch of the surface might not have been covered in its hair or, worse still, malodourous droppings. Cohen busied himself preparing unrequested coffee which he poured, she noticed, into three mugs. Seeing her glance, he explained, 'One for you, one for me, and one for mother,' and then disappeared out of the kitchen to deliver a mug to another room. Alice made out only a quick, whispered conversation before the sound of a door slamming could be heard. Cohen reappeared, handed a mug to her and sat, in the armchair opposite her, gazing expectantly into her eyes. She sipped from the mug, noticing as she did so its crudity. The lip was so thick that any liquid drunk inevitably dribbled down the outer surface.

'I made it myself, you know. I do pottery though I'm a painter really,' Cohen volunteered.

Nature had not been kind to Roderick Cohen. He was pale and plump, and despite his evident middle age, his face was disfigured by a patch of red, angry-looking acne. He had lank, greasy hair and the beginnings of male-pattern baldness, producing in him a high oleaginous forehead terminating in a Draculaesque widow's peak.

'To business, Mr Cohen,' Alice said authoritatively. 'I think that on the evening of Thursday 1st December you had a drink in the Raeburn Inn?'

'Probably.'

'Could you be a little more precise, Mr Cohen? Can you recall whether or not you were there that Thursday evening?'

'I am there most evenings, but, yes, I think that I was probably there that Thursday.'

'Did you see anyone you knew?'

'Of course.'

'Sorry, what do you mean?'

'As I am there most evenings I know most of the staff and regulars.' He smiled triumphantly.

'Can you recall whether you saw Ian Melville that evening?' Alice ploughed on.

'Yes.'

'Yes, you can recall or yes, you saw him?'

'Oh Sergeant, you're so sharp! Yes, I can recall I saw Ian Melville that evening.'

'He's a friend of yours?'

'Sort of. He's a bit of a babe-magnet, so I usually go and see him if he comes in. You know, get the crumbs from his table.'

'Had you arranged to meet that night?'

'No. He came in and I gravitated towards him.'

'Can you recall when he came in?'

'Now, that is difficult. I wasn't completely plastered, so it'd probably be early evening. Maybe seven or eight.'

'When did he leave?'

'I have no idea. I left before him.'

'When did you leave?'

'At about nine, I think. I went to a club, I remember that alright! Do you ever go clubbing, Sergeant?' It sounded unpleasantly like an invitation.

'No,' she responded firmly, noticing with horror that the slight show of authority had, if anything, widened the ever-present grin that seemed to have been tattooed onto his face. The grin vanished only when an old lady shuffled into the kitchen, clad in a bathrobe and slippers, and replaced her mug on one of the units.

'Mother, if I were to say to you, go away, important business is being conducted in here, how would you respond?' Cohen spat angrily at his parent.

'I'd say bog-off, Roderick,' the old dear responded cheerily, before exiting in her over-large mules.

Unflustered by the public rout, Cohen returned his attention to Alice.

'And, Sergeant, if I were to say to you, would you like to see my studio, how would you respond?'

Alice managed to bite back her immediate, truthful reaction and substituted instead an inoffensive, anodyne one.

' Very kind...' she lied, '...unfortunately, I've no time. I'm expected back at the station about now.'

So saying she rose, and as she did so Cohen did too, somehow effortlessly managing to intrude into her personal space and transfix her with his glassy, fish eyes. The smell of garlic became overpowering. Stepping backwards to recover the distance between them she walked out of the kitchen and down the corridor that led to the exit. An open door on the right revealed Cohen's studio, and she noticed, to her amazement, that the walls were covered in exquisite seascapes, all of places she knew: Tyninghame beach, Fidra, the Bass Rock, the view seawards from Tantallon, all in delicately executed water colours. A wonderful collection, catching light on water, the movement of the sea and the translucence of shallow waves.

'These are yours?' she said, unable to hide her surprise.

'Of course, what were you expecting?'

Out of kindness she lied again, making no reference to the mud-coloured female nudes she'd anticipated, and said only, 'Oil paintings.'

Elaine Bell's office was thick with the odour of Friar's Balsam, and as Alice entered it the DCI was coughing, like a dying consumptive, down the telephone receiver. As she listened to her caller she wrenched a cough mixture bottle off the sticky ring on her desk to which it was attached, removed the cap with the fingers of one hand and poured out a measure.

'No, please just tell them we're saying nothing, we've nothing to say, they'll get all the information they're going to get at the press conference.'

She looked up at Alice while listening to the response, and then finished the call. 'Over and out, Charlie. I repeat, please tell them just to be there, because they are getting nothing from any of us, on the record or off the record.' Stopping only to down the cough mixture she immediately turned her attention to her Detective Sergeant.

'Alice. Good. I needed to see you. A press conference at Fettes has been arranged for four pm and I'm supposed to produce the first draft of the statement, for revision by the press office, and I've not the time at the moment. Anyway, you're a graduate, so you'll be good at this kind of thing, and the one you did for the Muirhouse rape was excellent. The brass are desperate to make it sound as if we're making progress, though God knows we're not. I think you should attend the press conference too. The Assistant Chief Constable's in the hot seat this time instead of me, thankfully. Charlie at HQ wants a statement as soon as possible, and I've got to brief the boss on any development so that he's not eaten alive. How did you get on with the QC's widow?'

'A lot of useful stuff. In particular, it seems that the victims, Clarke and Pearson, did know each other…' Alice's speech was interrupted by another telephone call, and the DCI picked up the receiver while handing her a sheaf of notes and gesturing towards the door. She left willingly, her eyes now beginning to water from the pungent vapour, glad to return to her desk.

The draft release was, in its way, a masterpiece, containing lots of material but no real information. No reference could be made to the identical *modus operandi* or the presence of the scraps of paper in case special knowledge was needed at the trial or any copycats were spawned. Reference could be made to the existence of a suspect, but the fact that he roamed free and had not been arrested betrayed the lack of any confidence that he was responsible for the killings. In the absence of further investigations nothing could be said about any connection between any of the victims, and the fingerprint evidence had proved unhelpful so far. Consequently, only its existence, as opposed to its usefulness, could be mentioned.

Thus, Assistant Chief Constable Body was sent naked into battle or, at least, to swim with sharks. The creatures had already smelt the blood, seen the dancing trail of flesh particles and were intent upon finding the source and ripping out great mouthfuls of meat. Elaine Bell would have survived the ordeal; she had a world-weary charm that most of the press understood and appreciated, and was an acknowledged mistress of the non-offensive stonewall. She could do it beautifully, and the journalists seemed to accept that it was a legitimate stroke in their game, sanctioned by the rules and executed by a professional. She would have flannelled on about positive continuing investigations, the fact that a suspect existed, the need for co-operation and the assistance of the public and, crucially, it being 'early days'. Her pale face and hoarse voice might even have elicited sympathy in the few who had retained some human feeling. All her limbs and appendages would have been intact on leaving the water, even if nightmares followed the experience.

Laurence Body functioned well within a hierarchy, where everyone knows their place and deference is due to those above from those below, and where gold braid rather than brains can end an argument. But he was quite unable to cope with the free-for-all that the press conference became. He read his prepared statement in a monotone and then, looking anxiously at the faces assembled before him, invited questions. The first blow was struck by the giantess.

'So, at present, no real leads and no sound suspects?'

Body, brows furrowed, attempted to explain that this was simply an absurd summary of the information provided, as she would appreciate on re-reading the copy statement supplied. Mitchell then lunged for the jugular with an enquiry about any connection between the killings, or the absence of any connection, and the possibility that a serial murderer was on the loose in Scotland's capital, free to slay again. The large conference room was hushed as the Assistant Chief Constable responded.

'A connection between the killings has not been ruled out at this stage or... er... ruled in. Whilst, obviously, multiple victims are involved, there is nothing to suggest that a serial killer is... er... on the loose.'

And so it went on, with Body blustering away at one minute, reduced to silence the next, until, to the relief of those who disliked blood sports, the *coup de grâce* was administered by a confident operator from *The Times*.

'So, the probability is that the killer remains at large. One who has struck three times in the last ten days. No one has come forward as a witness to any of the crimes. No useful forensic leads currently exist. No suspects have been arrested. Would that be an accurate summary of the state of the investigation to date? If not, perhaps, you would like to take this opportunity to correct it.'

Body made no response. Instead he ostentatiously collected his papers, switched off his microphone and acted, to all intents and purposes, as if no question had been asked. Following a whispered conference with his neighbour, an underling was despatched to switch the microphone back on and announce, to the stunned gathering, that the time allocated for the question session had now expired.

9

Monday, 12th December

The report from Stratheden was nowhere to be found. Elaine Bell's hand scrabbled through the chaotic sheets of paper on her desk, searching frantically for it. Before jamming the phone between her head and her shoulder, she unclipped one sheet from another, read the lower one to herself and, sighing with relief, picked up the phone again, ready to speak.

'I've got it now, Sir. I have to say that neither of the DCs who went to the hospital gained the impression from the staff that they considered Peter Bennett to be capable of the crimes we're concerned with, despite his past record with knives. However, I do accept that he was out at the time of the McBryde killing. They say he suffers from…', she looked down at the sheet of paper and then continued, '…"severe personality disorder", and about ten years ago attempted to cut a woman's throat. Since then he's been on a high dose of tranquillising drugs, shuttling between Fife and Carstairs and receiving "cognitive and behavioural therapies", whatever they are. The doctors seem to think that he's safe now, at least as far as others are concerned. The worst thing he's done of late is to pour a bowl of his own bodily fluids over a fellow inmate. The shrink in charge is a Dr Nicholson. I'll get the number for you from Holmes and fax on the report he…' She stopped, listening to a lecture from the other end, and then finished her sentence '…sent to me, to you at HQ. Of course, I'll accord this part of the investigation top priority, Sir. '

Putting down the phone she held her head in her hands, closed her eyes and exhaled deeply. Everyone was working flat out, every stone was being turned and now, somehow, men had to be found to traipse back over the Forth Bridge to check up on a loony who could not possibly be responsible for the Clarke or Pearson deaths, even if his M.O. did include throat-slitting. Thy will be done, anything to keep the brass off her back. She picked up a packet of paracetamol and looked at her watch. Another fifty minutes to go before any relief from the next duo of tablets, fever or no fever.

Alice knocked on the Chief Inspector's door and edged in without waiting for a summons.

'Yes?' Bell said wearily, looking up at her.

'I have some news that could be described as good, I think, Ma'am.'

'Go on, Alice.'

'Well, as I said before, Alastair and I visited Laura Pearson and got some useful stuff. She was in a bit of a state, so we didn't get that much from her directly, but she gave us the name of a good friend of her husband, Alan Duncan, a Silk. He was extremely helpful, telling us that about five or six years ago Pearson and Clarke were lovers and were both involved in a road traffic accident which resulted in the death of a child. It seems to me that the parents of the child might want their blood, mightn't they? Duncan also said that Laura Pearson must have known about the affair between Clarke and her husband, but she told us, point blank, that her husband didn't know Elizabeth Clarke. To be fair, she was pretty emotional at the time, but we'll have to go back and see what's going on.'

'I agree, Alice, but you'll have to tread very carefully. I've already had my ear bent as a result of a complaint from Pearson's mother-in-law to the Assistant Chief Constable. She says that you treated her daughter as a suspect and harried her. All we need now is an official one...'

'But it's bollocks! Complete bollocks. If that's how Mrs Winter imagines suspects are treated then she can't have read a book, been to a film or watched television for decades. The spoilt old witch...'

'Alright, Sergeant, alright. Calm down, I believe you,' Elaine Bell pacified her subordinate. 'Just remember, please, that we're treading on eggshells as far as the Pearsons are concerned. I've got enough on my plate without thunderbolts from on high directed at us by the old... dear. There are some in the force, as you know, whose day, no, whose week, would be made if that kind of cock-up were to occur, and I, for one, would rather not find myself teaching road sense to under fives or comforting battered wives again. Now, I think you and Alastair should go to Fettes to check up on the road traffic accident. OK ?'

'I can. Alastair can't as he's off ill, mild flu or something, but he should be back tomorrow with luck.'

'Go with Sandy Moray then.'

'He's off too, Ma'am. Flu.'

The clerk from the records department at Fettes deposited a large pink file on the desk, apologising as she did so that the computers were still down, and explaining that the IT department had it in hand. Alice leafed through the file, extracting black and white photographs of the accident locus and a hand-drawn plan showing the locations of the vehicles from a bird's eye view. A black cross marked the impact site, the spot where the child had fallen, and the cars involved were represented as rectangles. Stapled to the front was a typed statement, date-stamped 3rd June 2000, given by David Pearson:

> 'Statement by David Pearson, Advocate, 'Drumlyon', Merchiston Place, Edinburgh, given to PC Jay No. 5220.

On 3rd June 2000 I was a passenger in a BMW car, registration no. PSG 555, driven by Dr Elizabeth Clarke and heading from Gullane to Edinburgh. At about four pm in the afternoon we entered Macmerry on the old A1 road. As we approached a stationary ice-cream van, parked opposite a 30-mph sign, a child ran out from the front of the vehicle. Dr Clarke immediately braked and swerved towards the centre of the road, but she was unable to avoid colliding with the child. We got out of the car and Dr Clarke attempted to minister to the child. The boy was unconscious and lying on the road. I believe that immediately prior to impact, and after applying her brakes, Dr Clarke was travelling at about 20 mph or so. Visibility was then good and the road conditions were dry. Before he emerged from the front of the van the child was not visible.'

A statement from Dr Clarke was attached to it, couched in similar bland police prose, although the consultant provided a fuller description of the circumstances of the accident, noting:

'...I saw the stationary ice-cream van from quite a distance away and was aware of the potential risk to children on a main road. Accordingly, I reduced my speed to about 15 mph. Just before I reached the midway point of the van I noticed a child running from the bonnet area across my path. I immediately applied my brakes and swerved to the right but I was unable to avoid striking the boy. I stopped the car and ran to the child. He was lying face upwards and was unconscious. I was unable to feel any pulse and noted a large contusion on the child's forehead. A haematoma had already begun to appear in that area and I formed the view that he had probably suffered a skull fracture. I ensured that he was not moved until the ambulance arrived...'

The date stamp was also 3rd June 2000. Two additional accounts were contained in a brown envelope, one given by the driver of the ice-cream van, a Mr Royston, another from a woman who had been walking her dog at the scene, a Mrs McIntyre. Both witnesses stressed that, in their opinions, the driver of the car was not going too fast, estimating her speed at about 15-20 mph, and emphasising that she stood no chance of taking avoiding action. Mrs McIntyre stated that she blamed the boy's parents and that children of his age should not be allowed out unaccompanied to cross roads. Mr Royston described the boy as 'just a wee laddie', noting that he was 'too young to be out alone'.

The accident investigation form revealed that the child had been aged five and was called Daniel David Spurgeon. His parents were listed as Ian Spurgeon and Jane MacVie, and an address at 'Redbyres Farm Cottage, Macmerry' was provided. In the middle of the file was a typewritten statement by Elizabeth Spurgeon of No. 4, Paton Road, Macmerry. She described herself as the dead boy's 'gran', and said that Daniel had been staying with her following some sort of row between his parents. She had been responsible for her grandson on the day of his death, and he had been crossing the road with his ice cream in order to return to her home. On the back of the file was stamped, in black ink, 'No prosecution', and as Alice was returning it to the counter clerk, a photograph fell out of it onto the floor. It showed a little boy, auburn-haired, freckled, smiling widely at the camera and exposing his crooked little milk teeth. She picked it up, dusted it and slipped it back into the folder, wishing she had never seen it.

No Spurgeons or MacVies were listed in Macmerry in the phone book. Alice left the motorway at the Tranent turn-off, climbing the slip road to join the old A1 with its wide view of the Firth of Forth shimmering in the weak winter sun. The countryside between the two towns was desolate: flat fields of sodden, yellow-ochre-tinted grass enclosed by windblown hedges, a few huddles of cold sheep sheltering in their lee. An assistant at the Co-op gave her directions to Redbyres Farm Cottage, and the Escort rattled like an old tin can as she drove along the muddy track that led to the edge of the disused opencast site and the cottage. The dwelling appeared to be occupied by some kind of radio ham. A huge mobile mast stood erect in the ill-kempt garden, in amongst two wrecked cars, wheel-less and propped up on bricks.

As she opened her car door a large black rottweiler, thick streams of saliva on his muzzle, jumped up at the chicken wire fence which acted as a stockade for the house. In immediate response to its furious barking a squat woman, with tightly frizzed coal-black hair and pencilled eyebrows, emerged from the cottage and walked to the gate. As the dog continued to growl ferociously, she squeezed herself through the gate, barring the dog's exit, cooing ineffectually, 'Doon Donna, doon, good dog, Donna,' all the while as the brute jumped up, clawing her tight slacks. Alice flashed her identity card and introduced herself.

'Ah've got a TV licence noo,' the woman said defensively.

'I'm sure you have, but it's not my concern. Could you tell me, is this Redbyres Farm Cottage?' Alice asked.

'A-ha.'

'I understand that a Jane MacVie or Ian Spurgeon live at this address. Are you Jane MacVie?'

'Naw, I'm Rita Ness.'

'Okay Rita, could you tell me does a Kenneth MacVie, sorry, Kenneth Spurgeon live here with you?'

'Naw,' the woman smiled, relief washing across her features, 'I stay here wi' my husband, Dennis, Dennis Ness.'

'Well, thanks for your help, and I'm very sorry that I troubled you. Could you assist me with one further thing before I go? Have you any idea where either Jane MacVie or Ian Spurgeon are living now?'

'Naw. We used tae git letters addressed tae them but they flitted, mebbe, aboot six year ago... Just aifter the wee boy was killed. We got the cottage then, ken. Dennis works on the fairm and I work in the big hoose fer the Baileys.'

'No forwarding address was left for MacVie or Spurgeon?'

'Naw, and I dinnae ken where they stay the noo.' The woman shook her head to underline her point.

'One last thing, do you know if Ian Spurgeon's mother still lives in the village?'

'Oh aye, she does. She stays in Paton Road. I seen her on her zimmer in the post office sometimes, but she's not richt noo, never has been richt since wee Daniel's death. Mind, it was her blame onyway, a wee boy like that. I couldnae live wi' masel if I'd done it, she as good as killed him hersel. Nae wonder her nerves are playing up. She should never hae let him go to the van himsel, she should hae gone wi' him...' The woman shook her head vigorously again before continuing.

'Are you a detective, hen? Need to be clever, eh, fer that job?'

'I am a detective, yes.'

'Then how come ye didnae ken that I wisnae Jane McWhitever? Ayebody here kens me.'

The heat in No. 4 Paton Road was stifling. The flames of a coal-effect fire were flickering away in the ceramic grate and two large radiators in the tiny sitting room were set at maximum. The old lady eased herself slowly back into an armchair and directed Alice to take a seat in the one opposite it. The television was on and orange-faced people were jumping up and down, participating in some kind of game show, supervised by a girl dressed in a chicken suit and harangued by an unseen audience. Alice attempted to speak, but was unable to make herself heard above the racket coming from the set and, exasperated, turned it off, surprising herself with her own impatience. She was about to apologise, but noticed that Mrs Spurgeon's gaze had not moved from the television, her eyes were still focused on the blank screen.

'I've just been to Redbyres Farm Cottage looking for your son and Miss MacVie,' Alice said loudly, hoping to get the old woman's attention.

'There's nae need to bawl, pet,' came back the cool reply.

'Sorry,' Alice said. 'We need to speak to him and Miss MacVie.'

'Is he in trouble again?'

'No, I don't think so. Where would I find him?'

'I dae ken. He's jist got oot o' Saughton. Ask the prison, they'll hae an address. He'll hae probably gone back to the wee bitch in Windygoul, but I've no' heard from him. He never even wrote me when he was inside.'

'Could I have... er... the wee bitch's address?' Alice asked tentatively. The woman moved her large bulk in her seat, finally shifting her gaze from the television and onto her visitor.

'I dae ken it exactly, like, but she stays in the East Windygoul estate in Tranent,' she replied.

'And... could I have... er... the wee bitch's name?'

'Sharon Calder.'

'And Jane MacVie, any idea of an address for her?'

'Oh aye, she sent us a Christmas caird. Mair than Sharon's aye done. It'll be on the mantle...', Mrs Spurgeon pointed to the collection of cards above the fireplace. 'I think she put her address in it. Just grab the lot o' they cairds and bring them here.'

Alice obediently gathered up the fifteen or so Christmas cards from the shelf and deposited them in the old lady's lap. She worked methodically through them, before extracting one depicting a crudely-drawn, swaddled Christ child smiling wanly at the world from a pink background. Glitter had been dropped inexpertly onto patches of translucent glue on the card in an attempt to spell 'A Merry Xmas', but only every second letter seemed to have been hit by the silver rain. Inside it, in large childish writing, was inscribed 'Crist's blessings be with you, Gran, at Christmastide and forever. Love Jane.' The dots above each 'i' were circles, and at the top right-hand corner there was an address, 'Helives, 22 York Place, Kinross.' As Alice was noting it down, the door of the sitting room was flung open and a little girl came skipping into it, singing at the top of her voice, followed by a woman pushing a buggy containing a toddler. On seeing Alice the child in the buggy began to wail loudly as if confronted by a ghost, and his sister, now stationary, cowered behind the television set. Alice collected her bag and left.

Tranent is less than three miles from Macmerry, and East Windygoul was not hard to find. The estate was a cold slap of a place, pebble-dashed houses set on meat-red brick foundations, with tiny gardens and old crisp packets and sheets of soggy newspaper instead of flowers. The first person Alice stopped to ask where Sharon Calder lived turned out to be deaf, and the second was, as she somehow expected, a stranger to the area. When, finally, she found the house, the electric door-bell was hanging off the wall and her knocking brought no response. She moved on to the neighbouring house and rang the bell, being pleasantly surprised to be greeted by a smiling man.

'What can I do for you, bonny lass?' asked the pensioner in a strong Newcastle accent.

'I'm looking for Sharon Calder,' she replied.

'She's away at her work. She'll not be back until… oh maybe… ten or so this evening. She's a barmaid. You'd get her tomorrow, though, it's her day off.'

'Is Ian about?' Alice asked. The old Geordie's expression changed immediately.

'That bugger… he'll not be returning here, I doubt. No

better than a fucking animal, that one. Should be kept caged up forever.'

The Christmas lights of Kinross were a largely token affair. On every fourth lamppost a tiny white light guttered shyly as if ashamed to draw attention to itself, and spread across the High Street was a festive holly chain with one red berry and a centrepiece composed of a green parrot, flapping morosely from side to side in the wind. The local supermarket roof sported a collection of bulbs that flashed at random, spelling out nothing in particular. York Place formed part of a new development that straggled through Sandport down to the shores of Loch Leven, housing the executives who commuted daily to Edinburgh or Glasgow. Every door had a brass number attached to it, and above No. 22 was printed 'HE LIVES' in capitals, the house name. As Alice stood at the open door a voice from inside shouted 'Enter', and, mechanically, she obeyed, passing through an unlit corridor to the source of the voice in the kitchen. At a round table two people were seated, a bearded man and a middle-aged woman with grey hair scraped into a bun, from which thin wisps escaped. Bubbling on the stove was a huge vat of some kind of stew; great big orange squares of turnip rotated in a sea of grease, and tide-marks of brown gunge were visible on the ladle protruding from the pan.

'Just help yourself,' the woman said, rising to get her visitor a bowl.

'Thank you very much, but I've already eaten,' Alice said quickly, eyeing the unsavoury hash.

'I was looking for a Jane MacVie. I understand that she lives at this address?'

The woman looked concerned. 'Why? Why are you looking for Jane?' she demanded.

Alice took her identity card from her coat and showed it to the pair. 'I'm sorry,' she said 'I should have explained. I am

Detective Sergeant Alice Rice of Lothian and Borders Police, and I need to find Jane MacVie to talk to her.'

As she was speaking, an old man entered the room and sat down at the table. Wordlessly the woman handed the bowl she had got for Alice to him; he ladled some of the greasy sludge into it and began to eat with noisy pleasure.

'You alright, Jim?' the bearded man asked. The new entrant nodded, intent on his meal and nothing else. The woman sat down at the table again and said:

'Ms Rice, we run an open house here, we help anyone that comes to us for help. Our food is their food, and such shelter and warmth as we have, they have too. All for His sake. Jane lives with us now. What do you want with her?'

Alice could feel her anti-Christian hackles rising. Any overt displays of religiosity had this effect on her. She'd met too many whited sepulchres in her time, and her convent education had, inadvertently, transformed her into a die-hard sceptic.

'I am sorry, I didn't catch your name...' she said, by way of a reply.

'That's because I didn't give it. Julia. Julia March.'

No ring visible.

'Well, Miss March...'

'Mrs March,' she was corrected instantly.

'Well, Mrs March, I need to speak with Miss MacVie in connection with a road traffic accident that occurred in 2000 involving her son, Daniel.'

'2000 is a long time ago, Sergeant. What can anybody possibly want with Jane on that painful subject after such a long interval of time?'

'That will be explained to Miss MacVie when I see her,' Alice said firmly.

The woman's hostile expression did not change, but she shouted: 'Janie... Janie, there's a lady to see you.'

As Alice waited for Janie to appear, she looked around the room. It was anarchic; on the floor along any free wall space there were piles of bedding, and beneath one heap of blankets a pair of white feet protruded. A sleeping bag, apparently occupied, blocked the fridge door, and a pair of worn socks dangled from its handle. Janie, when she arrived, was a pathetic sight. Unwashed fair hair clung to her brow and fell, in chewed strands, over her shoulders. Her face was pale, lardy-white, and her lips seemed bloodless, like those of a corpse. She looked drugged.

'I think I'll speak to Miss MacVie on her own. Is there another room available?' Alice enquired of Mrs March.

Ignoring the thrust of the question, Mrs March enquired of Janie, 'Janie, do you mind seeing the policewoman on your own?'

Janie shook her head and Alice followed her heavy-footed waddle out of the kitchen to a bedroom, smelling strongly of talcum powder and unwashed feet and littered with clothes. In the absence of chairs the Detective Sergeant and her interviewee sat side by side on the unmade bed.

'Miss MacVie, I wanted to speak to you about... well... firstly, the accident in 2000.'

'Yes.' The reply was strangely toneless.

'After your little boy died, did you and Mr Spurgeon leave Macmerry?'

'Yes, yes, that's when we left.' She paused, and then corrected herself. 'No, sorry, that's not right. That's when I left. Ian stayed on. I came to Kinross as I had a friend here. Then I found Jesus and He saved me.'

'So since Daniel's death you have lived in Kinross?'

'Yes... I went to the church and I met Julia and Bob. They took me in when my friend lost her house and I've lived here since. I help, you know... I make the soup, wash up, things like that.'

'Do you drive?'

'No.'

'Would you mind telling me where you were on the evening

of Thursday 1st December between about five pm and nine am the next morning?'

'I don't remember, but I'd be here. I'm always here.'

'What about Monday the 5th December between about four-thirty pm and eleven-fifty pm?'

'Like I said, I'd be here.'

'What about Wednesday 7th December…'

Janie cut in impatiently. 'Here! I'm always here. This is where I stay… I never go anywhere else.'

'You didn't go to Edinburgh on any of these dates?'

'No. I told you I'd have been here, in the house.'

'Were you on your own or with others?' Alice asked.

'I'm never on my own now. I can't be. Julie and Bob are always here, and if they have to go out then someone else comes in to watch me. I can't be on my own since Danny died. I tried to do away with myself after it happened, got took to hospital and they pumped me out. I think about it, about Danny, all the time. Sometimes I have to cut myself to make it go away.' She rolled up the sleeve of her tracksuit top to reveal a forearm covered in thin white scars, cut after horizontal cut from wrist to elbow. Then, pulling the cuff down, she continued, 'They look after me, Julia and Bob and the others and Christ the Lord, my saviour.'

Alice persisted. 'Mr Spurgeon, Ian, what happened to him?'

'I don't know. Before Danny died he liked a drink, but afterwards he was always smashed, drunk out of his mind. He had a go at me a few times, knocked my teeth out.' She opened her mouth to show a space where her two front teeth should have been. 'It was just the drink really, I loved him to bits, but I couldn't cope with that. Gran said he'd nearly killed a boy in a pub in Leith and got took to Saughton for it. It was in all the papers, like, but I never seen it and I never visited him nor nothing.'

'Gran?'

'Ian's mum. She lives in Macmerry with Ian's sister and the two grandkids.'

Alice decided to change tack. 'Do you remember the names Elizabeth Clarke or David Pearson?'

'I'll never forget them... they're the ones that ran over Danny. Never prosecuted, like, even though they'd killed my wee boy. Julia told me that they're both dead, said it was in the papers. She even showed me, but I didn't read it. I've forgiven them anyway, I forgave them when I surrendered myself to Jesus.'

In the kitchen Bob was sitting reading religious pamphlets. He confirmed that Janie had been in the house on the nights that the killer had been at work in Edinburgh, and that it was true, she never left the house and was never alone in it. As Alice rose to leave he handed her a leaflet entitled 'God: A Brand New Tomorrow', and asked leave to say a prayer over her. Christ Almighty! she thought, railing against the selfishness of Christians who determined to detain others, however hungry or exhausted those others may be, in order to relieve themselves of their urge to worship. She nodded weakly, and as Bob fell to his knees, self-consciously she did the same.

'Lord, bless Miss Rice and all her work. Let her dispense her earthly justice with your guidance and grace...'

Thinking the blessing was over and wonderfully speedily at that, Alice was just about to rise to her feet when the voice resumed: 'Keep her free from sin in this unclean life, let her turn the other cheek in accordance with your word and let honesty and a love of truth inform her every action.' Two further minutes of devotion followed, and then, at last, the end: '...for Jesus Christ our Saviour's sake, amen.'

The Indian carry-out in the polythene bag was leaking, dripping pink slime onto the unwashed stairs that led to Alice's flat. She stopped on Miss Spinell's floor and waited until the final chain was freed. Contrary to her expectation, Quill was not liberated to run, jumping and barking, to greet her but, instead, she was ushered in. Miss Spinell was annoyed. She explained, strangely cold in manner, that the forces of law and order were failing in their statutory duties, as further thefts from her premises had occurred. On this occasion, things had been removed from her bathroom: yesterday no soap, today no shampoo. Where would it all end? she demanded. With me in the loony bin too, Alice thought, but she bit back her riposte, saying only that she would inform her superiors and that scene of crime officers might attend soon. Usually, the promise of action soothed the addled old lady, but tonight it appeared to cause further irritation. Had Alice forgotten so soon? The thief had already removed Miss Spinell's Sunday gloves and would, obviously, be wearing them, so scene of crime officers would be a waste of time, as there would be no fingerprints left by the villains. Thinking only of the tandoori chicken and basmati rice in the leaking bag, Alice explained that the force's new positron intensifier would be used, a machine which could find prints even if gloves were being worn. Miss Spinell was mollified, and as Alice tipped her rice onto her plate she reassured herself that sometimes, just sometimes, dishonesty was the best policy.

IO

Tuesday 13th December

Every year Edinburgh is taken by surprise when it snows, as if the stuff has no business falling so far south and on the capital at that. Its annual presence fails to dislodge the city fathers' belief that their metropolis is a snow-free zone, requiring no special precautions, no special measures, a site untouched by winter and its cold heart.

When Alice awoke, the city had undergone its yearly transformation and Broughton Place was carpeted in white, a surface undisturbed by anyone or anything, a virgin field awaiting despoliation by its residents on their way to work. Looking out of her bedroom window she watched as little eddies of snow rose from the church roof at the east end, only to fall, spilling like icing sugar onto the sparkling surface below. She dressed quickly in a thick woollen jersey, jeans, boots and an old skiing jacket. The collar and lead were slipped over Quill's neck and they set out for their pre-dawn walk. Inverleith Park was deserted, and the dog, freed from its lead, spun round and round in circles, chasing his tail and puffs of snow, barking loudly and revelling in his own speed and energy.

By eight am the peace of the snow-bound city had been shattered, its smooth covering replaced by chaos and its silence by an angry, impotent roar. Broughton Street, a small incline leading upwards from London Street to one of the main arteries of the capital, had been closed to all comers. An articulated lorry had jack-knifed across it by the Catholic Apostolic Church, smashing a bus-shelter and turning the road into a dead end. The traffic on George Street was moving at a snail's pace, led by a bus crawling from stop to stop with a retinue of desperate drivers in its wake, each praying that the one in front would not brake too suddenly on the untreated, treacherous rink. Even The Mound was impassable, its underground heating system failing on its first call into service of the year. The roundabout at the top of Leith Walk was at a complete standstill: thick, white, exhaust fumes filled the air from the queues of trapped vehicles, each one revving ineffectually at the slightest sign of any advance. And Princes Street itself was blocked; a black cab, wheels spinning uselessly, showered the nearby pedestrians with a fine spray of slush. In short, the city had been disabled by the snow, found wanting, unable to cope, as if confronted by the unexpected demands of monsoon rains or hurricane winds.

Alastair was at his desk, his long fingers clamped around a mug of steaming tea, clasping it to his chest as if it was a hot water bottle. Inspector Manson was also in the office, leaning against the coffee machine and sipping from a polystyrene cup, a chocolate biscuit in his free hand. As Alice approached he sneezed noisily, rocking himself with the impact and spilling the contents of his cup onto her.

'Sorry,' he said. 'You were in the wrong place at the wrong time, dear.'

'Not to worry, ' she replied evenly, 'I'll send the dry cleaning bill on to you.'

He smiled, watching her intently as she dabbed her breast with a hanky.

'Was the meeting with Dr Ferguson any use?' she asked him, her head still down attending to the stain.

'Total waste of ruddy time for all concerned.'

'Nothing at all, Sir?'

'Well, let me see... He knew Dr Clarke and didn't like her. He described her, and I quote, as "another stuck-up bitch". He was convinced that she didn't rate him highly enough professionally, didn't recognise his true genius. He said that the only reference she'd ever written for him was lukewarm at best, more communicated by what she didn't say than by what she did. But that was all. Nothing deeper. Like all the others he conceded that she was a good doctor, caring etc, but too stand-offish with the rest of the staff. Also, she was unable to delegate, he said, to him at least. He appeared genuinely shocked when I asked him if she might have had any connection with the black market in hospital drugs. Seemed to think that butter wouldn't melt in her mouth. So, as I said, a total waste of police time, my precious time. I hear your trip to Kinross wasn't any better.'

Alice shook her head, 'No, not completely valueless, Sir. I think we can now safely exclude Jane MacVie as any sort of suspect, but that still leaves Ian Spurgeon in the frame.'

'Don't hold your breath, dear,' Manson said, licking a crumb from his upper lip, 'all roads still lead back to Melville, mark my words.'

Having swallowed his mouthful the Inspector sneezed again, trumpeting like a charging bull elephant and spilling the remnants of his coffee onto the floor.

'I'll drive,' Alice said, moving towards the driver's door.

'You must be joking, it's like a skating rink out there,' Alistair replied.

'So?'

'So, maybe I should drive today.'

'No thanks, I'll be fine.' As if it had been an offer.

Alistair stooped to fit himself into the car, knocking his head on the central mirror and cursing as he tried to find the seatbelt.

'What's been happening since I've been off?'

'You should be off now. You're still sniffing and I'll catch it.'

'Keep your window open.'

Alice began to wind down her window and icy air swept through the vehicle. She continued until the last sliver of glass became invisible.

'You have no mercy… Please, please shut it, you're not in peril. But what has been happening?'

'Not much really. Cohen was a rare freak, just the thought of him makes me shudder, and not with pleasure before you suggest it, and he gave me nothing except the creeps. I suppose Melville's still odds-on, though I'd put money on that it wasn't him. Photos of him were shown throughout the Medway to no avail, and McBryde's workmate, Davie something or other, didn't recognise him.'

'Anyone got anything on McBryde from his family?'

'No. DS Travers traced his mother to an old folks home in Portobello, but she was away with the fairies and thought that Sammy attended the Queen, you know, polishing her crown, feeding the corgis etc.'

'There must be something, surely?'

'Not at the moment. I met up with Jane MacVie and she's found her Saviour, so she'll be turning the other cheek. No bloodlust there, and two evangelicals corroborated her story. The boss is wearing herself out, sneaking out for fags and downing cough mixture like sherry.'

Alice coughed, unable to speak, and then glared at her partner. 'I've caught it already!'

He did not respond to the joke, but answered seriously.

'Alice, do you find this one gets to you? It gets to me. I keep seeing that poor doctor's blood on her ceiling, and the smell of Pearson's post mortem seems to have stuck in my nostrils. I feel this bastard's presence, his anger, fury even, and I'm sure, somehow, he's dying to do it again. Usually, I'm OK. You know, not too bothered, but…'

'Me, too. It's as if he can do whatever he likes and we just follow, as if we've got hooks in our mouths and we're on his line. When I close my eyes to sleep I see the wound in Pearson's neck. Don't know why, I've seen enough gore in my time… but it's the one that keeps coming back.'

Large snowflakes had begun to land on the windscreen of the Astra by the time they reached the coast at Musselburgh, and they continued to fall until the car had strained up the brae that leads from Wallyford to Tranent. Then, as abruptly as it had all begun, the snowfall ceased. Tranent seemed to have fallen asleep under its white blanket; chimneys smoked and lights shone, but all its inhabitants were safely wrapped up indoors. When the pits closed the place closed too, and precious little of the spoils of that dirty industry ever filtered back into its dark streets. No grand public buildings or monuments had been erected there, courtesy of any of the black barons, just a miners' welfare club and a Masonic Lodge. Before the bypass all the traffic on the A1 rumbled through Tranent, creating the semblance of a pulse, but its beat had disappeared with the opening of the motorway. No heart was pumping now, no life left, the sleep of the dead.

At the Brig Inn they turned right, slithering down the untreated slope by the disused coal-railway towards the collection of shuttered workshops that led to Windygoul. The snowy weather had been unexpectedly kind to the estate; beneath its immaculate covering the usual detritus of litter, cannibalised car-parts and dead grass were concealed.

Sharon Calder's door was opened by a smartly dressed young woman, bent double, holding the collar of an Alsatian to prevent it from jumping up on the callers. She explained to them that she was Miss Calder's social worker and was just leaving, but that she would go and see if her client was prepared to talk to the police. Alice patted the coarse hair of the dog as they waited patiently in the hall before being shown into a sitting room. Sharon Calder was there, reclining on a sofa with her slippers off, breastfeeding her baby. To shield herself from their gaze she adjusted her cardigan, obscuring all sight of the child. She was pretty, with downward sloping green eyes and soft brown hair, but appeared prematurely careworn; fine lines already corrugated her forehead and bracketed her mouth. Over her left eye was a massive bruise, blue-black in colour and extending up into the temple and down over the cheekbone. It had begun to heal, its dark border merging into yellowing skin.

'Does Ian Spurgeon live here?' Alice asked.

'Not now,' Sharon Calder replied.

'Have you any idea where he is living now?'

'I don't know where he stays, permanent like, but I know where he is. He's in hospital in Haddington, the Roodlands Hospital, with two broken arms.'

'How long has he been in there?' Alice persisted.

The girl looked at her social worker inquiringly. 'Maybe since… eh… 28th November. That'd be right, eh, Miss Short?' Her companion nodded her head and Sharon Calder went on. 'Aye, he got out on the 26th, came here on the 27th and the boys done him over on the 28th. I mind it was then, I had an appointment at the clinic.'

Alastair spoke. 'Would you mind explaining to us what happened?'

The girl looked down at her baby, stroked its head and then continued without lifting her eyes from her child.

'Ian was in Saughton, but youse'll know that already. Went in maybe late 2001. He moved in wi' me after Janie left, poor cow. I felt sorry for him and all, losing the wee boy and everything. When he went inside I visited him regular, wrote letters, done everything I could and it wasn't easy getting time off work, expensive too with all those buses. By the end I'd got to know the place really well, knew some of the wives, like I was one of them. Then I made my big mistake, I got friendly with a boy, had a few drinks and fell pregnant to him. Course, he didn't want to know me after he found out I was expecting. Next time I sees Ian he knows all about it, I'd told one of the girls and she'd passed it on to her man and he'd told Ian. But Ian was great. I'd expected him to shout at me, bawl the place down but he was fine. Said it was all okay, we could still be together and that he'd treat the child like his own once he was out...'

She stopped and pressed the child more closely to her before continuing. 'Jesus! If that's how he'd treat his own. He came here on the 27th and seen the baby, took her in his arms and gave her a great big smacking kiss. I thought it was all going to be alright, that we'd be a family like, him, me and the bairn, 'cos he didn't seem angry or nothing, just glad to be out and happy to be with the two of us. Next day he came back from the Brig, about tea-time, and he was steaming. He had a go at the both of us, grabbed the baby off me like she was a doll or something and flung her onto the settee and then started hammering me, kicking, punching and all the while screaming that I was a whore at the top of his voice. Mr McSween from next door heard him and came running in. He managed to pull Ian off me, even though he's an old man and then Ian turned on him. I picked up the baby and ran to my Mum's and we locked the door. One of my brothers was in the house and he phoned Alec, the eldest, and then the two of them went into my house and beat the shite out of Ian. Mr McSween got the police and Alec and John were taken to the station but they're not being charged with nothing. Ian got took by ambulance to the hospital, lights flashing, both his arms got broke in the fight...'

'He'll never beat up a woman or a child again,' Miss Short said quietly.

Sharon Calder carried on. 'He's got both arms in a stookie, ken, plastered, the now. A friend of mine works as an auxiliary in Roodlands and she told me, said she'd heard the doctors discussing his injuries and they said he'd be lucky if he could lift a pint when he got out, the boys had done such a thorough job on him.'

The appointment was for four-thirty pm and must be kept, Alice knew that. To distract herself she looked around the dentist's surgery, scanning the drill, the little basin, the tooth colour charts, flitting onto the shiny autoclave, and then her gaze inadvertently landed on, and became transfixed by, the dentist's hairless hand, thumb balanced on the plunger of the hypodermic, free hand flicking the full cylinder. And the needle. The needle seemed to go on forever, designed surely to penetrate the armour-plated skin of a rhinoceros, not her soft, pink, throbbing gum. Fighting against the urge to leave, and obeying a command, she opened her mouth and felt only a sharp jab instead of the excruciating pain she had braced herself to withstand. Every muscle and sinew relaxed, and she listened to the drill at work as if it was in someone else's mouth rather than her own. A quick wash with the pink liquid and she was out, face frozen, hamster-cheeked, and a small stream of saliva running unstoppably from the side of her mouth, but with no further appointments for six months.

A fat Santa Claus, having escaped from his grotto for a fly smoke, winked at her, reminding her that Christmas was coming and that all her shopping remained to be done. Maybe even making a pass at her. Despite the weather, the stores were full, crammed with people milling about apparently aimlessly, looking for inspiration in amongst all the tinselled tat. Briefly she joined the throng in a clothes shop, wandering amongst the pullovers and socks until she came to, determined to make a list and do all her shopping in a single, well-executed strike.

At home there were three messages on her answerphone. One was from the DVD shop to inform her that *Delicatessen* was four days overdue, one was from her sister reminding her that her brother-in-law's birthday was in two days time, and the third was from Anthony Hardy. It was short and to the point as usual.

'Hello. It's me. Fancy a drink tonight at Colliers? Phone me if you're not going to make it. Otherwise I'll see you there at six-thirty.' They had known each other for years, had met in a cold lecture theatre and clicked immediately. For all of a minute Alice contemplated staying in, visualising a long, luxurious bath followed by a diet of mindless television, and then, snapping out of it, she went to change.

An open fire was blazing in Colliers and Anthony had secured the table nearest to it; he was engaged in erecting a house of cards out of dog-eared coasters and did not see her enter. It was clear that he'd come straight from the Advocates' Library; his work clothes were visible beneath his overcoat and his shiny black lace-ups stood out amongst all the slip-ons, moccasins and scuffed trainers lined up along the bar and clustered together by the giant television screen. An unsmiling barman gave her the glass of white wine she'd finally been able to order and she moved to join her friend at his table. He looked up, gave her a brotherly kiss and then stared morosely into his dram.

'It's happened. I've finally broken up with Andrew,' he said. It was no surprise to Alice. His relationship had been on the edge of the abyss for months, teetering dizzily between renewed passion and despair, and she had provided a sympathetic ear throughout it all.

'I'm sorry. When did it happen?'

He sighed. 'Yesterday. Well, yesterday we decided that we would split up, but we've been trying to work things out, as you know, since May. I can't talk to him any more, he says he can't talk to me either. Every time either of us speaks, the other misunderstands it. It's got to the stage that we hardly dare say a word in case another argument starts. Funny, because it used to be so easy, we were always talking, always had things to talk about...', he shook his head miserably. 'I don't know what we're going to do. We've lived together for such a long time and everything's so inextricably mixed. We've agreed custody of the cat and the dog and I'm getting both, thank God. I've known for ages that this would happen, but now that it has I don't know what to do. Obviously, we'll have to sell the flat, and I suppose I'll look for somewhere else in the city. Andrew's away at a conference in Leeds so I'll have the place to myself tonight.'

'You told me, last time in the pub, that you thought he was seeing someone else. Was he?'

Anthony took a sip of his drink. 'I don't know for sure…', he ruminated. 'In a way it doesn't make much odds. If he was it was because he wasn't happy rather than the other way round. He keeps saying that there's no one else, and, on balance, I believe him. I think I'd rather it that way, that our relationship had just worn itself out. I don't want to be replaced immediately. God knows I looked long enough for Andrew, and for all his faults I don't think I'll ever find anyone half so lovable. It'd be galling to see him out with someone new too soon. Now I'll be quiet. You've listened to all my worries enough times before. We'll switch to you. How's your love life, sweetheart?'

'Cruel of you to ask. I've had to resort to desperate measures. Again.'

'Well…' he said coaxingly, '…tell me.'

'Only if you promise, promise, solemnly promise, not to tell another living soul?'

'Okay. I promise.'

'I've answered another ad in the *List*.'

'No! Alice,' he said, incredulous, 'you must be joking!'

'Just desperate. You've no idea how hard it is, Anthony. I never meet anyone, at work I only come into contact with policemen and they are all very well in their way but… all my old friends are married and only do things with other married people, the single men I know—and you're a case in point—are either gay or nothing. Any new man is snapped up by some ever-ready piranha lady long before I become aware of his availability.'

'What did it say?'

'What did what say?'

'The ad! The ad! What else?'

'Mmm. Hard to recall the exact wording. Something like "normal man would like to meet",' she laughed. 'Christ! It's all too corny and pitiful. Imagine a world where "normal" can be taken as a recommendation. But it's true. Remember the last one that I met, the bus driver from Bathgate? His claim to fame, success or whatever, was that he'd paid off the hire purchase on his car, and "stocky" turned out to be Sumo fat, but on paper he managed to make himself sound like... well... a catch. Anyway, the die is cast, and we're to meet tomorrow, somewhere safe in broad daylight. You can afford to laugh, it's much easier for you, Ant. You can go to clubs and...'

'No,' he interrupted her. 'it's not easier and I hate the club scene, in fact, the whole gay scene. You know that. Apart from Andrew I'm the only straight gay man I know, and I don't think there are any hang-outs for people like me. Half of my straight friends are camper than me. Talking of answering ads, did I tell you about the one I answered?'

'No.'

'I'm sure I did tell you about it. No? Well, the advertiser was called Jim, I think, Jim or Tim, something like that. It was all hideously embarrassing. He turned out to be a solicitor and we'd even met before, professionally, at a conference on the tax implications of damages. He recognised me immediately, and would like to have scarpered, I could tell from his face, but he didn't, and we spent an awful hour or so together exchanging inconsequential rubbish in a seedy bar until I gathered up enough courage to leave. Never again! Never again! Too many lies can be told on paper, and I wouldn't trust myself on one of those voice-mail like things. God, to think I've got to join you in the bear pit... Anyway, I have some splendid news.

Remember that awful case I told you about, the lady who hoovered up her own nipple?'

'No.'

'I know I told you about it. Have you been using aluminium pans again?'

'I'm sure you didn't. It's not the kind of thing I'd forget.'

'Oh well, I had this case involving a lady who had a mastectomy and woke up, as you do, with only one nipple. In such circumstances, the medical men had come up with three options to "replace" the missing item. You can get artificial ones which you glue on, you're provided with a box of them apparently, or you can get permanent tattoos or, finally, some kind of skin graft using material "harvested", as we say, from the inner thigh, as it's nicely pink. Well, this lady's hoovering her carpet one morning, her nipple falls off and in a flash it's up the Dyson…'

'Hang on one minute, Ant. Was she hoovering in the nude or something? How come it didn't fall off into her bra or blouse or something?'

'You're so literal. She was—', he stopped in mid-sentence to answer his mobile phone. As he listened, his expression changed and his voice, when he spoke, was subdued. Alice had little doubt that the speaker was Andrew. She went to get more drinks, and to show his disapproval of women customers, the barman catered for all the men at the bar, latecomers included, before turning his attention to the first-comer, Alice. And once the dinosaurs ruled the earth, she thought to herself, watching him as he slowly attended to her order with undisguised distaste. On her return to the table she found Anthony with his chin cupped in his hands.

'I've got to go, darling. I'm sorry. Andrew changed his plans and caught a plane this evening so that we can talk things out properly. Again. I can't see that it'll help, but it was good of him to even think about it. He'll have had a hellish day speaking to all those doctors, and I should think the last thing he wanted was hours of travelling on top of it. He's at the airport now, and I said I'd get there as soon as possible to pick him up. I'm really sorry to end things so abruptly. Maybe we could have a drink later this week or early next, and I could hear about your date?'

'Don't worry. Off you go, next week or whenever would be great. There's only one thing I need to ask you, Ant, it's my work. I'll be really quick. Did you know David Pearson?'

'Slightly. Not a friend of mine or anything, but I know exactly who you mean and we've chatted occasionally in the gown room. Are you working on that case?'

'Yes, but I'll tell you about it later, when we've time. What was he like?'

'Seemed pleasant enough. A womaniser, I think, but not prone to discussing his conquests in anatomical detail unlike some of the others up there. I heard, in the Faculty rumour factory, that he was having it away with some fairly newly called female. I'm afraid I can't remember her name. But you know how unreliable the gossip there is.'

'Ant, is there any computer programme in the Faculty which can produce the names of cases involving particular expert witnesses and Counsel?'

'Yes. You can get that information quite easily.'

'Would you do me a favour and provide me with the names of any cases featuring Dr Elizabeth Clarke and David Pearson?'

'I could do better than that. I'll get copies of any judgements in any cases in which they were both involved. Would that help?'

'Sounds perfect. Could you let me know as soon as you've had a chance to look? Would you also find out the name of Pearson's latest conquest? It might just be useful.'

'Yes, I'll aim to do both things tomorrow. Life's a bit busy at the moment, so I can't guarantee it, but I'll do my very best. Got to go—Andrew will be waiting, and I don't want to make things worse than they already are by being any later than I have to.'

On her own, Alice nursed her glass of wine, taking occasional small sips and enjoying the warmth of the fire. It would be interesting to see those judgements, if there were any. She would learn a bit more about Elizabeth Clarke, if nothing else. Nothing on Sammy McBryde, though, he would still be the odd man out. Perhaps she should have asked for the search to include him, but, she thought, he had no connection with the courts, with the law, a long shot to put it mildly. Nothing lost by it, though. For a minute she considered phoning Anthony to add McBryde's name to the list, but picturing his perilous domestic situation she decided to wait until tomorrow. The rest of the evening, now it had been handed back to her, could be spent in Granton Medway. Maybe DCI Bell would think it a waste of time, but it was her time to waste.

At the first house she rang the doorbell in vain. Light was visible from between twitching curtains and a TV was on, but no-one was answering the door, or not to her, at least. The second house was inhabited, the door opened and a little child peered round the edge of it, joined in seconds by a teenage girl with a towel wrapped like a turban around her wet hair. As the girl explained that her mother was out at the bingo, a male voice from behind her shouted out that 'the whole fucking CID' had already been round, and that 'cunts' like Alice should be out catching the serial killer, not wasting decent people's time.

And so it went on, quiet hostility at best, vocal abuse at worst. At ten pm she decided to call it a day and walked back to her car, cursing the hubris which had made her revisit such a depressing hellhole, when she already knew that the solid industry of all the uniforms had produced nothing. On impulse she stopped to watch a skinny little boy as he skateboarded under a streetlight on the icy pavement. He had made a course out of a series of little wooden ramps, and flew over them, time after time, in a breathtaking display of aerobatic grace. He seemed unaware of the presence of his audience, absorbed in his own elegant performance. Landing for the last time, he packed his board under his arm and seemed about to leave. Alice clapped and he looked up, conscious for the first time of his onlooker and pleased to have his skill recognised.

On impulse, she spoke. 'You didn't happen to see anyone you hadn't seen before at Sammy McBryde's house on the night that he was murdered, did you?'

'Mm. Aye,' he nodded his head.

'You did see someone there?' Surprise had made her slow.

'I jist said so, didn't I?'

'Can you tell me what the person looked like?'

'It wis a man. He wis dark, I think. He had dark hair like and he wis carrying a polybag.'

'How tall?'

'He wis a big guy, a tall guy, bigger than my dad.'

'How tall's your dad?'

'He's a right big man.'

'Was the guy fat or thin or just in between?'

'In between.'

'Was he white or black?'

'White.'

'Can you remember what the time was when you saw him?'

'I dae ken. I wis in ma room, we stay opposite Sammy and Shona's hoose. I wis watching the TV. That programme wis oan, the yin wi' the burds what decorate yer hoose. It must hae been after seven. I wis just looking oot o' the curtains.'

'Did you tell the constables this when they came round?'

'Naw.'

'Why not?'

'Naebody asked me. I telt ma mum after the polis had

gone, but she said it wis too late. They'd already told the polis they'd not seen nothing.'

'What was the man wearing?'

'Cannae mind. It wis dark. Jeans, I think, jeans and a jacket.'

'What was the man doing?'

'Calling on Sammy.'

'Did the man go in?'

'Aye. He went in and then Sammy shut the door.'

'Did you see anything after that? Did you see him leave?'

'Naw. I watched the TV and then I went to ma bed.'

Alice could have hugged the child, kissed his pale cheek. It was something, not a lot, but something. The killer was a man, a tall, dark-haired man. She would like to have rewarded her assistant in a currency he would appreciate, a new skateboard, new kneepads, new helmet, but she had nothing to give, nothing except further praise for his virtuoso performance, and she heaped it on, until she sensed that he had begun to think that she might be a nutter. Despite the late hour, when she got home she e-mailed Alastair.

'Went to Granton Medway tonight. Spoke to a boy who the uniforms missed. An eyewitness. Seems our killer is male, dark-haired and probably over six foot tall. Remind you of anyone on our books? I wondered whether we should go and see Ian Melville again. What do you think? We could go first thing tomorrow. See you there at nine am?'

An answer came back almost immediately.

'What are you on? Don't you ever give up? Anyway, well done. See you at St Bernard's Row at nine am. We'd better let DCI Bell know what we're up to, so I'll go to the station first thing. Have a good sleep, Sherlock.'

II

Wednesday, 14th December

Flora Erskine woke and with consciousness came, again, the feeling of dread, a sensation of acute anxiety which she felt would never be allayed, would be with her for always. How simple and easy things had been before David's murder. Every day must have been accompanied by hope, only she hadn't recognised, or valued, it at the time, but its absence was unmistakable, making everything that was colourful, colourless, and everything vital, dead. She lowered herself out of bed slowly, feeling as fragile as if she had a hangover. She found her white silk blouse and black jacket and skirt without difficulty, and rummaging in her tights drawers she pulled out holed pair after holed pair before settling on one that had nothing more than a slight gash in the underside of one sole. She'd see to it later. Already the familiar pain behind her eyes had arrived, as if the effort of keeping back the tears was too much for them, the pressure building up inexorably and unbearably. Today was going to be even worse than yesterday. She was scheduled to appear in court, and every appearance was still nerve-racking, an ordeal from start to finish, even when she felt at her most equable.

When she first began devilling she had carefully sketched on a piece of paper the positions she had to adopt at the Bar, standing on the right-hand side for the pursuer and on the left-hand side for the defender. Any mistake and inexperience was apparent, vulnerability exposed. She had tried to master the tortuous terminology used before the Bench, with all its subtleties, euphemisms and codes. So important to prefix things known with 'As I understand it…', in order to prepare for the revelation that the supposed fact was, in fact, incorrect. Crucial to remember to 'be obliged' to the judge for any assistance rendered by him, or for any order granted or even refused by him, even though in the case of refusal the words had a sarcastic ring. Fundamental always to substitute 'I regret that I am unable to assist my Lord any further' for 'I don't know'—any admission of ignorance, legitimate or otherwise, being as unprofessional as the wearing of a pink wig. No doubt, one day, she would be able to speak the arcane language effortlessly and expertly and exchange 'If my Lord is so minded' and the rest of the flowery nonsense with the best of them, but, just now, the use of such such unnatural and confusing terms required unbroken concentration. She didn't feel like breakfast. A cup of coffee with four sugars would have to do.

She left the house to walk to work. The sun was out and the wet pavements shone in the bright light like mirrors; all of yesterday's snow had melted in the overnight rain and the sky was a deep, clear blue. The day could not have been more beautiful. She recognised its magnificence, but felt none of the elation that such beauty normally evoked in her. The interminable inner monologue that she now conducted involuntarily with herself occupied her until she reached Parliament House. Had she told him that she loved him? He could have been in no doubt. Would it have mattered to him anyway? Yes, because it would have mattered to her. She had been so absorbed in her thoughts that she had not been aware of leaving the New Town, climbing the Mound or crossing the busy High Street.

The ladies' gown room was surprisingly full for a Wednesday morning. At least eight members were searching for their wigs, adjusting their gowns and jostling for a view of the only two mirrors. Mrs Shaw, the gown room assistant, was busily sewing on a missing blouse button and, for once, her CD player was silent. As if to compensate for the loss, she was humming 'Shall we dance' in a loud, mechanical drone, her head bent over as her needle and thread worked their way through the white material.

Flora knew that she had been the subject of gossip; she was conscious that her affair with David Pearson had been considered state of the art tittle-tattle, replacing even the fevered speculation about the sexuality of the latest judicial appointment. Maria had told her that the cat was out of the bag after attending her last stable dinner. At the gathering her friend had been quizzed by at least three of their male colleagues, in various states of intoxication, about Flora's 'affair'. Each had adopted a different approach; the first, and boldest, had spoken of it as a fact, daring Maria to deny it if it was untrue. The second had inquired, in tones of sympathy, how Flora had become entangled with such a rake, no doubt hoping that Maria would not recognise the assumption, implicit in the question, of the existence of the affair, and would inadvertently confirm it. The third, unmistakably rat-arsed, simply propositioned Maria, suggesting that with 'Flora and David' they'd make a fine foursome.

As Flora knew that she had not breathed a word to anyone apart from Maria, upon whom she could rely, David must have been indiscreet, maybe even boastful, and the thought made her cringe as she began to envisage what he might have said, who he might have told. She was as sure as she could be that no one had seen them together in any circumstances other than those which could be satisfactorily explained by work. But her fellow members were observant, fluent in body language and with memories like elephants for any smut doing the rounds. It was not as if she had not been aware of his reputation before they appeared together in the Mair case. That knowledge should have forewarned her, but, in some strange way, it had disarmed her because he had behaved so differently from the stereotypical philanderer she had imagined.

She had anticipated arrogance, flirtatiousness and, on refusal, unpleasantness. Instead, he'd seemed diffident, shy even, and had appeared genuinely disappointed when she had turned down his first tentative invitation to dinner.

She walked purposefully to her locker, extracted her white wig from the black and gold box in which it was kept, unhooked her gown from its hanger and then waited patiently for Marianne Edgecombe to finish her toilet in front of the mirror. As usual the woman carefully collected all the unruly strands of red-gold hair from beneath her wig to pin them up, before, as if there was all the time in the world, reapplying, to her already immaculate make-up, more mascara and more lipstick. While she was carelessly hogging the mirror, others attempted to straighten their wigs in the little reflecting glass left. After two minutes Flora gave up waiting for the endless retouching exercise to be completed, and went instead to use the mirrors in the loo. Remembering her holed tights, she searched in the cupboard below the sink for a spare black pair, and on finding an unopened packet she quickly changed into them, disposing of the damaged ones in the wastepaper basket. As she left the loo she checked her wig. It was fine, sitting straight at mid-forehead level and, so far so good, no tears. Yesterday her eyes had been permanently bloodshot, and she had muttered, in response to the few discreet enquiries their state had elicited, something about the itch and irritation caused by her conjunctivitis.

In the library she collected Burn-Murdoch on Interdict, Robinson's *The Law of Interdict* and the annotated volume of the Rules of the Court of Session. She then went out to the hall to perch on the fender by the great fireplace, to wait for the tannoy to announce her case and to watch her colleagues striding up and down as they gossiped or discussed their business. Just as her thoughts had involuntarily begun to drift back to David, she heard over the tannoy 'Court 6. Interim Interdict before Lord Lawford: Agents—Wright, Elgin and Brown.' She returned to the law room, grabbed her papers and books and ran to the modern courtroom. Disliking an audience, she was pleased to see that only one member of the public was present, a black-haired man who glanced furtively at her as she entered the room and then, as if displeased by what he had seen, immediately turned his head away, crossing his legs and facing the wall.

The Senator was still on the Bench, two young Counsel arrayed in front of him. She listened as he ruthlessly exposed the weaknesses in the argument of the one addressing the court. The anxious advocate was clasping the lectern on which his notes rested so tightly that all his fingers had blanched. An ill-concealed smile was present on the face of his opponent. He must be even greener than me, she thought. Sure enough. After he had risen to his feet he hardly had time to finish his first short submission before he was interrupted from on high by the sort of remark designed to chill the blood of the most experienced Counsel.

'Mr Swan, I have the advantage over you. I appeared for the pursuer in High versus Norton, the case upon which you seem to be founding, and it was purely concerned with quantum of damages. I fail to see what possible assistance it can be in any consideration of the relevancy of the pleadings, and that is, surely, the only question with which we are concerned today.'

Mr Swan, not yet capable of reading the writing on the wall, simply recited another long extract from the same case report, apparently oblivious to the meaning of the Senator's remarks.

Finally, Lord Lawford's patience broke and he bellowed: 'Unless, Mr Swan, you have any other authorities you wish to bring to the attention of this court, I might as well tell you that I intend to grant Mr Rose's motion on behalf of the pursuer.'

'No, my Lord, I am content to rely on High versus Norton,' came the now desperate reply.

'Very well. Pursuer's motion granted. Mr Rose, you will, no doubt, be seeking your expenses.'

On hearing the expression 'expenses', Flora moved towards the Bar in readiness for her own appearance. At least, at this stage of the proceedings in her case she would have no opponent. She attempted to stop her hands from shaking, and for the third time re-ordered her papers. Lord Lawford would not have been her choice of judge. No one doubted his brilliance or his misanthropic tendencies. Female humanity was rumoured to rank particularly low in his estimation, and within the Faculty it was believed that he had concluded that the Bar was going to the dogs and that it was his duty to frighten away as many new members as possible prior to his retiral. To that end, no holds were barred; the simple bludgeoning with irate words, the stiletto thrust of the missed House of Lords' case and the Delphic monologue which convinced its victim that he no longer understood English. All had been tried and tested by the newly elevated tyrant. Flora forced herself to speak, and as she was doing so she realised that, contrary to her earlier fears, she could not be embarrassed, could not be hurt. Her secret dread of breaking down in public was groundless. How could any of this matter compared to David's death? What could the bewigged figure on the bench say to her that could wound? Nothing whatsoever.

Emboldened by her new invulnerability she made three confident submissions in favour of the granting of interim interdict to her client, a tenant farmer from Argyll. She explained that the landlord's unauthorised removal of gates from the meadowhead field had resulted in the entry of ten Highland cows into the tenant's poly tunnels and the destruction of all the young plants therein. She was not harangued, she was not even interrupted. She was asked one polite question, to which she was able to give a sensible reply, and the interim interdict was pronounced in her client's favour. As she squeezed out between the benches, clutching her authorities and papers, she was patted on the shoulder by her instructing solicitor, his face creased with delight at the good result, but it all passed her by. She found she was as unmoved by success as she had expected to be by failure.

At lunchtime she went to the nearby Boots in Cockburn Street to collect newly processed photos. Image after image of David. The tears that had been held back with such effort finally made their escape and she took refuge in a nearby sandwich bar. With dismay she noted that there was only one empty seat in the whole place, and it was next to Colin Harvey QC. She would have retreated, but he had already caught her eye, smiling in recognition to signal the space. On spotting the tear stains on her face his embarrassment became evident, and she was at a loss as to whether to attempt to pass them off as some kind of allergy or to blame them on a death in the family. Without time to think she muttered something about her hay fever. For the next twenty minutes she dabbed her eyes and, as if a pact existed between them, they discussed the pollen count in winter and the most effective non-soporific antihistamines.

Her two o'clock consultation passed quickly. Flora knew from the sheaf of papers that she had already seen that little could be done to help Mrs Davie. The client herself hardly said a word, sitting, ostensibly unmoved, as Flora and her strident instructing solicitor discussed the case. Mrs Davie's only child, Kylie, had been taken into care by the local authority, and they had now applied to free the child for adoption. Mrs Davie did not want to lose her offspring, she did not want her daughter adopted and would not consent to such a course. The hearing was for the court to decide whether to dispense with the necessity for her agreement to the adoption procedure, but in order to fight the local authority they would have to have some ammunition. Kylie, now aged three, was already showing signs of severely disturbed behaviour: she was smearing her own excrement on the walls of the three-roomed council flat in which she lived, was almost completely speechless and spent hours sitting next to the washing machine, banging her head on it. In her short life she seemed to have developed every childhood disease known to the medical profession, and infestation with a rich zoo of lice, worms and other parasites. While Mr Davie had been part of the 'family unit' she had, in unexplained circumstances, also suffered a fractured skull and a burn to her left leg. Fortunately, Mrs Davie's last precognition stated that he no longer formed part of the family.

The woman appeared to have had the benefit of any and all parent-craft classes available and she was, as the entire Social Work Department admitted, always willing, but, sadly, never able. The explanation was simple. Her IQ was too low to enable her to look after a child, she could barely function at the level of a child herself and was illiterate, innumerate and incapable of caring for anyone. She was also pregnant. None of the psychiatrists approached so far on her behalf had been prepared to support her cause; the child's paediatrician and general practitioner both believed that adoption would be in Kylie's best interests; Mr Davie was now consenting to it and all the carers involved in 'the Davie case', without exception, were of the view that Mrs Davie was unable to look after Kylie.

Flora looked at the dejected specimen sitting opposite her. The woman's eyes, through their milkbottle-bottomed spectacles, never met her own, flickering restlessly from the central light to the water flask and back again. Her hands, resting before her on the table, had thick stubby fingers with nails chewed to the quick, old blood visible where loose skin had been bitten off. She might as well have had 'loser' tattooed on her forehead.

'You'd like to keep Kylie?' Flora asked her. She needed to know how her client would respond to cross-examination.

'Aye.' The dull-faced woman nodded.

'Can you explain why?'

'I love her tae death. She's ma bairn.'

'Do you think you would be able to look after her, if she was returned to you?'

'Aye, wi' help, I done it afore.'

'But you've had a lot of help so far, and even with it you were unable to cope with Kylie?'

'I've not had enough, I jist need that bit more.'

'But you've had all that the Department say they can give you.'

'Aye, fair enough, I'm getting better at the cooking and that.'

'So, you had difficulty coping with Kylie when she was on her own and now you've got another child on the way. How do you think you'll manage with two?' She knew she was pressing on the knife, but their opponents would show no mercy.

'We'll get on fine, I ken whit I'm doing noo. The twa of them'll play wi' each other and Kylie can look after the babby, help wi' its bottle an' all, gie it boiled sweets 'n other treats.'

'You don't think it'll be more difficult giving Kylie the care and attention she needs with a new baby in the house?'

'I'll hae Ron there to help me too, mind.'

'Ron?'

'My husband, Ron Davie.'

'I thought he'd left, I thought you'd split up for good this time?'

'Naw, naw. We've got back tigether, he's in the hoose the noo. He'll gie us a hand, he's the dad after all.'

Flora looked enquiringly at the solicitor to see whether she had been aware of this development, but she shook her head, signalling her own surprise at the change in Mrs Davie's household.

'And does Ron still think it's okay for Kylie to be adopted?'

'Aye. He says it'll gie us mair time for the wee un when it's born.'

'And is that true?'

'Eh... aye, but Kylie'll be a guid wee helper. She can help wi' the nappies and everything.'

'Is she out of nappies yet, Kylie herself?'

'Naw. I took them off her the once but she jist made a mess, so I put them back.'

With every question the impossibility of successfully defending the action became more certain, as time after time the mother had to rely on her mantra, 'But she's ma bairn and I love her'. No one could doubt the truth of the statement. The woman, despite her intellectual inadequacy, was fighting with every tool available to her to try to keep her child. She had refused to give up 'the bairn' in the face of heavy pressure from the Social Work Department to do so, she had defied her violent husband and, somehow, she had managed to contact a solicitor and explain her predicament to the professional. Her genuine affection for her child shone through, like an unquenchable flame, but it could not compensate for her total lack of competence in the most basic childcare. Flora's only armaments were to be bows and arrows backed up, maybe, with slings and stones; the Council, her opponents, were in possession of pump-action machine guns and full body armour. The sheriff would have heard it all before, and after the pathetic creature had been given her chance to sway the court the order to free the child for adoption would be granted. Mrs Davie would go on to have her next baby and, in all probability, an application would be made after a few years by the local authority for a freeing in relation to it, and so on and so on, until one day Mrs Davie would have her tubes tied. Unthinkable for Mr Davie, or his replacement, to have the snip and, of course, contraception doesn't work unless you have the wit to follow the instructions.

Flora walked home in the company of Katie Mann. Nothing more than chance had led to this; they were both going out through Door Eleven of Parliament House and heading for home in the New Town at the same time; but no better companion could have been chosen by kind fate. Katie suffered from intractable verbal diarrhoea, and for a conversation to continue only the occasional nod or shake of the head was required; she would do the rest, gliding from one long, complicated digression to the next, rarely returning to her starting point, the momentum of her enthusiasm making her overshoot it time and time again. The first topic, as they crossed Parliament Square, was fox-hunting, and they progressed to hair dye, the Isle of Man, the sleeping partner of the last Accountant of Court and, finally, the closure of the local clap-clinic, seamlessly and with minimal input from Flora. Digression followed digression in Katie's endless chatter, and Flora allowed the torrent of words to flow over her until, finally, they parted on Queen Street.

The phone rang. It was Maria. 'You alright?'

'Yep. I survived Lord Lawford, and apart from an undignified episode over lunch with Colin Harvey I managed to keep the tears at bay. How did you get on in Glasgow?'

'Fine, really. The professor behaved himself in the witness box, no mad speculation about suffocation despite the views he expressed at the consultation. The other side's expert witness hadn't seen all the child's records or any of the professor's reports, and wasn't familiar with any of the latest literature. He must have been duffed up horribly in a court somewhere, as he was afraid to answer any questions in cross-examination and just kept repeating that he'd made it all clear in the examination-in-chief. Since he was so unashamedly partisan, I reckon he deserved everything he got. We're back tomorrow, but we've only got one witness left. The sheriff wants written submissions, so we're reconvening after Christmas for them. All in all, better than I could have hoped for. I've prepared the stuff for tomorrow already, so I wondered whether you fancied going to a film?'

'I'd love to but I can't. I promised Rattrays that I'd get a Note on the Line of Evidence to them in a case that's already gone off the rails once, and I'll have to do it tonight as I've got two consultations tomorrow, so I won't have a moment then. What were you thinking we'd see anyway?'

'I don't really know, I'm open-minded. Maybe that arty Japanese ghost story or, possibly, the science fiction one about female humanity being descended from aliens as opposed to apes... You could choose. Go on, change your mind?'

'No, I must keep my nose to the grindstone. I haven't been getting through as much work as I should, as I keep thinking, obsessing, about David, but I'll have to sort myself out. Mortgage to pay, bank manager to nurse, self to feed.'

Flora returned to her desk. The written pleadings in the case, the Closed Record, made stomach-churning reading for anyone not familiar with the world of food production:

> 'The pursuer, Mrs Duff, worked in the evisceration department of the chicken processing factory. Prior to about 1999 there were eight different stages in the evisceration process, namely, transferring, cropping, vents, drawing, gizzards, lunging, neck cutting and neck cleaning. Transferring involved reaching up and hanging up chickens on shackles at shoulder or neck level. Cropping involved the taking of the windpipe and crop of the bird. Vents involved cutting the bird up the back passage with scissors and a vent gun. Drawing involved the removal of the insides of the bird using a drawing stick. Gizzards were where the gallbladder, liver and gizzards were removed. Lunging involved the use of a suction gun to remove the lungs. Neck cutting secateurs were used to cut the neck. These processes were carried

> out on a production line moving at the rate of about seventy birds a minute. In the latter part of 1985 the defenders installed neck cleaning, cropping and evisceration machines. Later they introduced transferring machinery. Following the introduction of this machinery the jobs in that department consisted of the following, namely neck slitting (involving the cutting of the chicken necks with knives), cropping, transferring, back-up (involving operatives putting their hands inside the bird and with a twisting motion pulling out the innards. This was required only when the machinery was faulty), lungs (involving pulling lung remnants off, the bulk of which had been previously extracted by machines), gizzards, skinning (involving the use of a "whizzo"), cleaning insides, neck cleaning and autotransfer.'

A plan of the premises had thoughtfully been provided with her papers showing machines described as 'featherators', and equipment which included 'the blood bath'. The case was worth buttons, a repetitive strain injury producing a two-week episode of carpal-tunnel syndrome in a woman on the edge of retirement. Tens of thousands of pounds had already been spent by the Legal Aid Board on pursuing it, and many more would have to be expended before the woman was rewarded with her paltry compensation. Reminding herself of the steady stream of work provided to her by the pursuer's agents, Flora attempted to rouse some enthusiasm for the case. She had just begun to apply her mind to the identity of the witnesses required for the proof—Mrs Duff herself, her three colleagues and their supervisor, the ergonomics expert, the orthopaedic consultant—when the doorbell rang. She left her study and went to answer it, thankful for the interruption; probably Maria calling to check up on her or trying to tempt her to go for a drink. She looked at her watch: nine-thirty pm, too late for the cinema.

While Flora Erskine was addressing Lord Lawford, hands behind her back, weight on her heels, written submissions disregarded with uncharacteristic *élan*, Alice Rice and Alastair Watt were being viewed with unconcealed rudeness by Paula Carruthers at Ian Melville's flat. Alice watched with amusement as the woman, whose terse greeting had disclosed a horsey, received-pronunciation accent, adjusted her manner on hearing Alice's equally rounded vowels, making it an iota more courteous. Paula Carruthers was unable to disguise her surprise at the voice answering her own—someone in the police force, of all places, with whom one might have been at pony club, teenage parties or, for heaven's sake, school. The obscure etiquette governing such a situation seemed to be too much for Carruthers' limited neurones, and she was unable to decide whether her visitors should be invited in, like friends or, at least, equals, or whether they should be required to wait at the door like Jehovah's Witnesses, delivery men and petty officials. As the woman continued to ponder her social predicament, Alice spoke again. 'It's Mr Melville, Ian, that we'd like to speak to.' Carruthers answered, still evidently preoccupied and decisionless, that he was in his studio and was not expected back until lunchtime at the earliest.

Melville's studio in Stockbridge was cold, colder than the street outside, and that was chilly enough despite the sunshine. An open door revealed a large space divided in two by greying bed sheets suspended from the ceiling, a rip serving as access between them. The sound of an industrial heater on the far side echoed in the place, producing noise but little heat, certainly insufficient to make any impact on the temperature in the place, which was more like that of a fridge than anything else. Any models foolish enough to disrobe would, if they did not pass out with hypothermia, exhibit blue-tinged flesh, matt with goose pimples. Melville's drawings were pinned up all over the bare brick walls: huge pencil or charcoal sketches of scantily clad acrobats, male and female, cavorting on the floor, revolving around pommel horses and flying, suspended in the air between two still swinging trapezes.

As Alice and Alastair were glancing at the pictures, Melville appeared through the rent in the sheet dividers and his previously untroubled expression changed, momentarily, to one of alarm on recognising his interrogators from earlier. As if he had not seen them he turned his back and crossed the room to a kettle, now boiling, and made himself a mug of Bovril. He was trying to keep the cold at bay in a thick jacket with some kind of fisherman's jersey beneath it and his hands were protected by fingerless gloves, their wool spattered with droplets of brightly-coloured paint. Still ignoring his visitors, he carried his mug to a junkyard sofa and began to drink, expelling puffs of white breath between sips.

'We want to talk to you about your whereabouts on the night that Sammy McBryde was killed.' Alice fired the opening salvo.

'You know where I was,' Melville sighed, 'I've already told you. I was here until about eight, and then I met Roddy Cohen for a drink. I was in the Raeburn Inn till ten, and then I went home.'

'Had you pre-arranged the meeting with Cohen?' Alice asked, knowing he had not done so.

'No. I came in and he was there. Either I joined him or he joined me, I can't remember which.'

'He's a friend of yours?'

'Not exactly. A drinking pal, at highest. Roddy usually attaches himself, like a limpet, to anyone in the pub that's in the company of a woman, in the hope of stealing her or becoming acquainted with any female friends in her trail. He sits and slavers and is, I suppose, rather gross, but he makes me laugh with his bizarre chat up lines and beseeching eyes. He's also about the best painter I know. He wouldn't perjure himself for me, if that's what you're thinking.'

'Was he still in the pub when you left?' Alastair asked.

'No. I think he'd gone earlier, so you'll have to take my word that I left at ten.'

'Did you go to Granton Medway at any time that evening?'

'No. I would have told you if I had,' Melville replied. He enunciated each word carefully, as if speaking to a particularly stupid child.

'You didn't tell us that you'd visited Elizabeth Clarke's flat on the night of her murder, until you were confronted with forensic evidence that made any denial useless,' Alice reminded him.

He smiled ruefully. 'That's true, and it was stupid of me. Maybe if you're ever in a situation like mine you'll find yourself behaving irrationally. The fear of being convicted of a murder you didn't commit does funny things to a person. All I can say is, I don't usually lie and I'm not lying now...'

Alastair broke in. 'A man answering your description was seen in Granton Medway on the night that Sammy McBryde was killed.'

As her partner was speaking Alice watched Ian Melville's face. The fear in his eyes was unmistakable, but fear of what? Being imprisoned for a crime he didn't commit, or for one he did commit? Somehow, he managed to keep his nerve, and his voice was strong, defiant even, when he replied.

'What am I supposed to say? I've already told you that I didn't know Sammy McBryde and that I haven't been anywhere near Granton Medway. I was at home watching the television when that man was killed. I know that as far as Elizabeth's death is concerned it looks like I had the opportunity to kill her and, in many minds, the motive too, but truly, Sammy McBryde is a complete stranger to me. Why on earth would I want to kill him?' He paused for a moment, looked his questioners straight in the eye and then went on the offensive, fuelled by anger. 'The papers seem to be suggesting that there's a serial killer on the loose. I am not a single killer, never mind a fucking serial killer. I wouldn't know McBryde, or Pearson for that matter, if they came up and shook my hand. You're wasting your time with me.'

A tall, dark man beside Melville in the line-up in the identity parade was sweating profusely; water glistened in the bright light on his forehead and neck, and he looked as if he might pass out with heat. Or guilt. Good, Melville thought, standing up straight, erect, shoulders back, chin up. The pose of an upright citizen with nothing to fear from the law, nothing to hide, the sort of person who co-operates with the police to the extent of assisting in line-ups to help them identify the guilty party. He willed himself to look straight ahead in an effort to catch the eye of his invisible accuser, to reassure the witness of his innocence and deflect him from choosing him.

Alice took her arm off the thin shoulder of the little skateboarder. He was shaking his head vigorously, eyes still fixed on the line-up of men before him from behind the smoked glass screen.

'Naw, naw, none o' they men, Miss. He's nae there.'

'Certain?'

'Absolutely positive, Miss. The yin I seen… naw, naw, he's nae there.'

12

Thursday 15th December

As she looked disconsolately through her wardrobe, Alice downed another gulp of the Chardonnay. It would help, give her courage, confidence, perhaps even bestow the gift of the gab on her or at least loosen her tongue. Taking a black pencil skirt from its hanger, she brushed off the few dog hairs clinging to it and tried it on in front of the mirror. She smiled at her own reflection, not because it pleased her, but rather in an attempt to lighten herself up. It would be important, her friends had told her, to look 'fun-loving' and 'up-for-it', but the effort required to maintain a carefree expression was too much, and she watched as her brows recovered their normal furrow and her mouth relaxed out of its obvious upward curve. She did not feel fun-loving or up-for-it, and her face would not lie, it reflected her preoccupation with the murder enquiry. She should be back in the office with all the others, leave or no leave.

The clock in the lobby of The Dome struck one o'clock, and people began moving lazily towards the dining area. The letter in her hand begged to be read again: 'You can't miss me. I am tall and will be wearing red boots. See you at one pm…' What had she been thinking of? What kind of freaky man wears red boots? What kind of woman wants to meet such a man? Her mind answered the question instantly and truthfully. A desperate one. The thought made her laugh, inwardly, at herself, and switching rapidly from panic and self pity to a sort of masochistic enjoyment, she imagined herself describing her rendezvous to Anthony. He would want to know every tiny detail, from the colour of her lipstick to the exit strategy she adopted. So she would have to observe everything, note everything, go through with it all, if for no other reason than to be able to tell him. Revived by this thought she felt herself smiling, an amused observer rather than a sweaty participant.

In an armchair at the other end of the hall another woman was seated. Clad elegantly in a simple grey suit, her long legs were placed gracefully to the side, revealing expensive, black stilettos. As Alice watched she noticed how nervous the woman was: her legs, always together, were switched from one side of the chair to the other and then back again, and her right hand was held close to her mouth as if the nails might be bitten at any moment. Every so often her lips moved, as if she was reciting something silently.

One-twenty pm. He was late, too bloody late, time to go. Alice rose and moved towards the doors. As she was doing so, she saw a man wearing red baseball boots making his way through the revolving doors. He caught her eye, and she knew from his smile that he had also recognised her. In order to leave she had to move towards him, and as she did so he began to extend his arms in greeting, robbing her of any opportunity to depart unobtrusively. Suddenly the woman in the grey suit appeared by his side, and put her arm proprietorially round his waist. He blushed, but made no attempt to disengage himself from the embrace.

'Up to your old vices again, Charles?' the woman said loudly, her eyes resting on Alice. The man shrugged; he appeared unable to move, like a fly trussed up by a spider. Alice did not know what to do. The man must be her date—how many men in Edinburgh would be wearing red boots in the very hotel where they were supposed to meet at the approximate time arranged? But who was the woman? Maybe an old flame, now a stalker, keen to embarrass her former love, in which case she could only feel sorry for him and, possibly, afraid of her. The man's looks were even within the bounds of acceptability, on first impression at least. The woman in the grey suit, seeing Alice's confusion, took control.

'No doubt you're responding to this chap's ad?'

Alice nodded, bemused.

'Well, to put you out of your misery, I can tell you that he's my husband. When he considers married life too dull he advertises himself, puffing himself beyond recognition I might add, and some poor sap usually falls for it. This time it's you. If it's any comfort, that's how we met. I replied to his ad, only then he was single...'

Cocooned in the back of the taxi Alice began to weep. The extent of her humiliation appalled her: to be all dolled-up to meet a sleazy adulterer, to be warned off by the wife, to be so needy in the first place as to look at a lonely hearts advertisement, never mind answer it. Tears fell, unchecked, down her cheeks. All she was trying to achieve was what the rest of humanity seemed to take for granted: a mate, a companion, someone to love. Through the tinted glass she watched as the married paraded themselves, in pairs, along George Street. Couples were arm-in-arm wherever one looked, not necessarily happy, but always together. Was it so much to ask that someone out there should have been made for her? She was shaken out of the deepening spiral of self-pity into which she was sinking by the jangling note of her mobile. It was Alastair.

'The fucker's struck again. All leave's cancelled and we're to go to the scene. DS Travers and some of the others are already there. Where are you?'

'In a taxi on George Street, heading home.'

'I'll meet you at your place. I'll leave the station now and see you there in about fifteen minutes. Okay?'

'Yes, fine. Do we know anything about the victim, who is it, who's been killed?'

'A female advocate, her name's Flora Erskine. Got to go. See you in Broughton Place shortly.'

Flora's friend, Maria Russell, had no criminal practice, had never had any criminal practice. The books of grotesque photographs routinely handed round in criminal trials involving violence were unseen by her and she had never read a single post mortem report describing the horrific injuries that one human being can inflict on another. Her field was consistorial law, matrimonial disputes involving children and, more often than not, money. Sitting on her friend's bed, out of the way of the forensic people below, she felt sick. The awful smell of blood had permeated the upper storey of the house, polluted it. And her mind would not let go of the image of Flora, throat severed, flesh gaping, her mouth hanging open as if in horror. How could any human being contain so much blood? How could such a thought have leapt into her mind? She wanted to curl up in the foetal position, close her eyes and block out the world, to pretend that the day had not started and begin it again. I must do something or I will start screaming and never stop.

She looked around and spotted a wallet of photographs on the bedside table and picked it up, letting the snaps fall onto the bed in a heap. She should have known, every one was of David Pearson, like a fashion shoot for a male model, except for the last, which depicted Flora and her lover standing, hand in hand, outside a hotel. She had taken that one, being complicit in their deceit, enjoyed vicariously their happiness. Feeling a desperate need to talk to someone, she picked up the phone and dialled her mother.

'Mum, it's me. I'm at Flora's house.' Her voice sounded dull, tired, on the edge of tears.

'Are you alright, Maria? You sound upset. What is it?' Her mother had, as she knew she would, immediately picked up her abnormal tone.

'Flora's dead. I found her this morning, she's been murdered. The police are here now, and I have to stay to speak to them…'. As she was talking, the door of the bedroom opened and Alice entered. 'In fact, I'll phone you later, I think they need to talk to me now…' She replaced the receiver.

'I thought you'd have a WPC with you,' Alice said, surprised to find a witness alone.

'I did. She had to go, they said someone else would be coming.'

'Have you had any tea?'

'I couldn't face it, thanks.'

'I'm sorry you were left on your own at all, it shouldn't have happened. I have to ask, Maria, can you tell me when you found Flora?' Alice asked.

'About… an hour ago.' The young woman's eyes were red, swollen with tears.

'What happened exactly?'

'I share a clerk with Flora, we're both advocates. Sheila, our clerk, phoned to tell me about a consultation fixed for tomorrow and said, in passing, that Flora hadn't shown up for a Summar Roll hearing, answered her phone or responded to her pager. That's very uncharacteristic of her, so I said I'd look in on her on my way up to the Faculty. I pass her door. So that's what I did.'

'The front door was open?'

'Mmm.'

'You walked in and found her, as she now is, in the sitting room?'

'Mmm.' She blinked, trying to hold back more tears.

'You phoned for us?'

'Yes.'

'Immediately on finding her?'

'Mmm. She was dead.'

'Did you see or talk to Flora yesterday?'

'Yes. We spoke on the phone. I didn't see her.'

'When did you last talk to her?'

'Yesterday evening.'

'When?'

'About seven pm. I rang to see if she'd like to go to the cinema with me.'

'When did the call end?'

'I don't know. Some time around seven-fifteen pm, maybe. We didn't speak for very long. I only know the time as I'd checked it to see what films we'd be able to catch.'

'And you didn't see or speak to her after that until you found her this morning?'

'No, that's right.'

Maria shifted her position on the bed and the photos on it cascaded onto the floor. Alice picked them up, looking at each one as she did so, and a cold shiver went down her spine. She handed one of David Pearson to the young advocate and asked, 'Can you tell me who that is?'

'David Pearson. A QC. The one that was murdered.'

'Was she having an affair with him?' She hardly needed to ask, the photos were confirmation enough.

Maria hesitated before responding. 'Yes.'

'Had it been going on for long?'

'I don't know exactly. I think it started soon after they were in the Mair case together. That went ahead in about June this year.'

'Do you know if his wife knew about it?'

'I've no idea...' she paused, and then continued 'I don't think she can have. Flora would have told me if that had happened.'

'Did you ever hear Flora mention the names Elizabeth Clarke or Sammy McBryde?'

'No...' she corrected herself, 'Yes. I think there was a female doctor called Clarke who was an expert witness, or something, in one of her cases. Maybe the Mair one, I can't really recall. But I have heard her mention the name, I'm sure. Sammy McBryde, that name's not familiar, and I'd have a reasonable chance of remembering it, as McBryde's my mother's maiden name.'

On the route to Merchiston Place and 'Drumlyon', Alice and Alastair discussed the approach they would adopt. Laura Pearson's promiscuous husband and his two lovers were now dead, and if anyone had a motive for killing the lot of them, Laura Pearson did. And she had lied about Elizabeth Clarke, denying any connection between the dead woman and her husband, even though she knew that they had been lovers for years. Pressure would have to be applied, could be applied with the kid gloves still on.

The widow opened the door, and her surprise on seeing the two police officers showed momentarily on her face, but she led them immediately into her living room. The CD of 'The Messiah' was taken off and packets of Christmas cards were cleared from the sofa where they were lying, in order to make space for the unexpected visitors. From her seat Alice studied Laura Pearson. She did not look like any kind of vengeful monster, more like a Carmelite recently released from her enclosed order and as yet unused to the world and its ways. A Reverend Mother, though. Appearances mean little, Alice reminded herself, thinking of the graveyard rapist and his resemblance to the archetypal angelic chorister.

Alastair began. 'We saw Alan Dunlop, your husband's friend. He told us that David had had an affair with Elizabeth Clarke.'

The woman bit her lip but said nothing, so he continued. 'When we asked you whether your husband knew Dr Clarke, you denied it.'

She shook her head. 'No, I just couldn't talk about it. I'm

sorry. I knew who could tell you anything you needed to know and I sent you to him. To Alan, I mean.'

'Alan might not have told us.'

'And the sun might not rise tomorrow. I know Alan, he loved David and he understands me. You needed information to help you find whoever killed Elizabeth Clarke and David, that's why you were there. I was sure Alan would tell you of their connection, he'd know as much about it as me, quite possibly more. Why would I deny something that was virtually public knowledge?'

'It being virtually public knowledge would mean, for you, virtually public humiliation?'

She flushed. 'Yes, and it did. But if you're suggesting from that statement that I would conceal the affair from you to avoid further such humiliation, it's nonsense. As I said I just couldn't, so soon after his murder, speak about that part of our life together. If you're suggesting that I hated David for humiliating me, you're right, but I got over it. Plenty of women do.'

'We also asked you about Sammy McBryde. Did your husband know him?'

'I told you, I don't think so. I can't guarantee it. I don't know exactly who he knew and who he didn't. All I can safely say is that if he did know him, he never mentioned anything about him to me.'

'And you. Did you know him?'

'No. I told you before that I didn't.'

'Can you tell us what you were doing between five pm and nine pm on Thursday 1st of December?'

'I don't know offhand. Can I look at my diary?'

'Of course.'

Laura Pearson went over to a low, walnut bookcase and extracted a small pocketbook from a red leather bag resting on it. She returned to her seat, flicking through the diary pages before answering.

'I must have been here. I can't have been out anywhere, as

my diary's blank and I'm meticulous about filling in any appointments, engagements and so on.'

'Would anyone have been here with you?'

'David, probably, unless he was still working at the library. No-one else. Our children visit occasionally but I don't remember any visit from them then. Mum was still away. She was on holiday in Sicily until the fourth of December.'

Alice broke in. 'Can you tell us where you were on Monday the fifth of December, between four-thirty pm and eleven-fifty pm?'

She looked in the diary again, found an entry, and responded. 'Well, for some of the time I was at a candlelit concert in Rosslyn Chapel—carols, given by a singing group called Rudsambee. It began at eight pm and finished at nine-fifteen pm.'

'Was anyone with you?' Alice continued.

'My mother, who you met, and my eldest daughter, Sara.'

'And before the concert?'

'They both came to tea, probably at about four-thirty pm or so. We had supper here before we left for Roslin.'

'What did you do when the concert finished?'

'We were all travelling together in the same car, my car. I dropped off my daughter in Liberton, then I took Mum to her house in the Grange and after that I came on here. I probably got back home at about ten-fifteen.'

'Was there anyone here with you from then onwards?'

'David was at home. I remember talking to him about one of the carols, "Il Est Né, Le Divin Enfant". He was particularly fond of it, and you don't often hear it sung nowadays.'

On the evening of your husband's murder you were here on your own. Is that correct?'

'Yes.'

'Where were you yesterday evening and this morning?'

'Between any particular times?' she enquired.

'Say, between seven pm yesterday evening and one o'clock this afternoon,' Alastair answered smoothly.

'Yesterday evening and yesterday night I was here on my own. I went shopping at about ten this morning, in Bruntsfield, other than that I've been here, on my own.'

'Do you know anyone called Flora Erskine?'

'No.' No pause. No flicker of recognition.

'Did your husband know Flora Erskine?' Alastair persisted.

'Well, it's a bit like Samuel McBryde. I don't think he did, but I can't be sure. He certainly never mentioned her name to me.'

Alice caught Alastair's eye. They needed a reaction. Alan Duncan had said that Laura Pearson was a very clever woman. Possibly she had lied to them before about her husband and Dr Clarke, although her explanation today for the lie would have been good enough to convince most juries. If she was ice-cool, then the ice would have to be broken.

'Flora Erskine was found murdered in her house, a little over an hour ago. Her throat had been cut,' Alice said, looking steadily at Laura Pearson.

The woman appeared puzzled, as if following a train of thought still being formed. 'And you think this killing is connected with the murders of my husband and Elizabeth Clarke…?' She stopped mid-sentence, panic in her eyes. It looked as if realisation was beginning to dawn.

'The connection… Flora Erskine and David were lovers?' she asked, a desperate hope for denial apparent on her face.

'We think so.'

'Dear God!' She hesitated, taking the information in before following inexorably the chain of logic leading back to herself. 'And you think that I am involved in their deaths?'

She looked up at Alice, her eyes fixed unblinkingly on the policewoman.

'I don't know,' Alice admitted. It was no more than the truth. Laura Pearson rose from her armchair, moved to the telephone, bent to pick up the receiver and then stopped. Without a word she returned to her seat, sat down and addressed her two visitors.

'As I am now a suspect in this case I was going to call a friend of mine, a solicitor, and I am going to do just that. But before I do, there are a few things you should know. After David's affair with that Clarke woman, he promised me that there would be no more—no more women, I mean. I chose to believe him. Our marriage could not have continued if I had not. That marriage produced three children and two grandchildren with one more on the way. I had to believe that David would not endanger that fine achievement, my only achievement, again. Now, you tell me that I was wrong, that he was having an affair with Flora Erskine, whoever she may be. All I can say, whether you care to believe me or not, is that I trusted my husband, accepted his assurance, and he gave me no reason to doubt him. I knew nothing of any affair with anyone and, as far as I am concerned, I still don't. I'll never get a chance to hear David's side of things, and there is no substitute, you two are no substitute. However, even if such an affair existed and I had become aware of it, I wouldn't have killed him, or Elizabeth Clarke or any other lover. I'd have divorced him, just like the majority of women do when they discover that they are lumbered with an unfaithful, lying spouse.'

After they had gone, Laura Pearson went into the kitchen and made herself some tea. As she raised the cup to her mouth her hand began to tremble, spilling the hot liquid onto the oilcloth covering the kitchen table. She lowered her hand carefully and replaced the cup in its saucer before cradling her head in both her hands and groaning. In countless situations when her nerve had been tested before, her sang-froid had never deserted her, and she would not allow it to do so this time. In every way we reap what we have sown, she thought, picking up her tea cup by the fragile bone-handle to take a sip and marshalling her thoughts for the conversation she was anticipating. In a matter of minutes she knew exactly what she would say, how she would respond to the likely questions, and what impression she would convey. She was now a suspect in a murder inquiry. Not just a suspect, *the* suspect, the prime suspect. Who, in truth, would be likely to have a more compelling motive? No, there was no shortage there. The police were bound to be back, and she must prepare. She must call Paul and enlist his sympathies, retain his services, ensure that all her armour had been donned; but first she'd have to collect Anna from nursery school and take her home.

'Can you hold, please?'

Before Alice had time to say no, the disembodied voice disappeared and was replaced by a tinny instrumental which she recognised, with growing horror, as 'O Isis und Osiris' from *The Magic Flute*. The piece had not only been shorn of the human voice but also speeded up, and her involuntary exposure to it, coupled with the unexplained delay, infuriated her. When the receptionist finally returned to the line, she could not have missed her caller's pent-up anger.

'Faculty of Advocates, how can I help you?'

'I need to speak to Anthony Hardy. Now.'

'Please hold while we try to find him.'

Again Alice seethed impotently as another few minutes passed. Finally, the chirpy voice reappeared. 'I'm afraid he's not responding to his pager.'

'Can you take a message for him, please?'

'Well, I'm not really supposed...'

'Thank you...', Alice cut in, ignoring the woman's protestations. 'Please tell him that Alice Rice called to ask, firstly, that he add the names Flora Erskine and Sammy McBryde to the computer search and, secondly, that he fax a copy of any details he can find about a case known as "The Mair Case".'

'I'll try and pass that on, but I've not got a pen and I'm only supposed to...'

'I am most grateful,' Alice said, and put the phone down.

Manson's smile alerted Alice to the problem long before he had opened his mouth. The smile remained, fixed and mirthless on his face as she swept past him towards the photocopier.

'Our good lady's baying for blood, Alice,' he said sweetly.

'No doubt we're all to be donors, Sir.'

'Nope,' he grinned in triumph, 'just blood groups Rice and Watt. I overheard her being savaged by the ACC, and your names and the words "out of control" and "serious repercussions" all appeared in the same sentence. Mrs Pearson's got Paul Wilkinson representing her, so she'll be bloody untouchable from now onwards, and that Winter woman, her mother, has been bending the Chief Constable's ear about your visit. You've certainly stirred up a hornet's nest. Anyway, dear, the DCI's just phoned to say she wants to see your good selves in her office now.'

The atmosphere in the room where the squad had assembled was heavy. Everyone looked tired and dispirited, and there was little of the chatter that normally accompanied such a gathering. Alice sat by herself looking out of the window, her eyes fixed, unseeing, on Arthur's Seat. She felt bruised. Maybe they had, as Elaine Bell had described it, 'galumphed in' like 'bulls on thin ice'. Maybe they should have been more cautious, more circumspect, in their dealings with the QC's wife, but their approach had paid dividends. Unless Mrs Pearson was an Oscar-winning actress, she could not have manufactured the look of surprise or despair that Alice had clearly seen on her face on hearing of Flora Erskine's murder and her husband's adultery. Alice had seen true emotion, not a simulation of it. The fact that the woman had understood so quickly the implications of the latest killing, the finger of suspicion now pointing at her, was, surely, a testament to her intelligence, not an indication of guilt. No doubt about it, Mrs Pearson was not the killer, but then who the hell was? The ACC entered the room followed by DCI Bell. As awareness of Body's entrance spread, the muted hum died down until there was complete silence. The DCI began her briefing:

'There's been another murder. It took place in the home of the victim, a girl aged twenty-five called Flora Erskine. She lived in a house in Dean Mews, own front door. Throat cut, again. A piece of paper was, as usual, left. This time the word's "untrustworthy", and we're back to lined paper and green ink. It had been placed by her head. The graphologists have confirmed that it's the same hand again. She was found dead this afternoon at about one o'clock by a pal, Maria Russell. Miss Russell spoke to the dead girl last night at about seven pm and, so far, it seems that no one saw or spoke to her after that. The same fingerprints have been found at the Mews as were found at Bankes Crescent and Granton Medway. A tall dark-haired man was seen by one of the girl's neighbours, George Hurst, leaving the Mews at about nine pm. Uniforms are still doing door-to-doors in the area and further information may be forthcoming soon. We've got the dog squad searching for a weapon, or anything else, as I speak.

Importantly, a connection between this victim and the last appears to exist. DCs Rice and Watt have discovered that Flora Erskine and David Pearson were engaged in an affair. Information to this effect came from the witness, Maria Russell, and seems to be confirmed by remarks made by Alan Duncan, Pearson's friend. Photographs of David Pearson were found by Flora's bed and their contents would be consistent with such a relationship. We already knew that Pearson and Elizabeth Clarke had, approximately five years ago, an affair. No connection, as yet, has been made between Flora Erskine and Sammy McBryde or either of the two of them and the doctor and the QC.

Ian Melville was under surveillance last night and this morning, and all his movements are accounted for. I've just put a watch on Pearson's widow. She may have an alibi for the McBryde killing, but she's got nothing covering the crucial times for her husband, Dr Clarke or Flora. So far, as you know, McBryde's the real mystery here in amongst all these New Town types. Laura Pearson's now got a lawyer acting on her behalf and I don't want anyone, and I mean anyone…', she looked sternly around the room, '…to talk to her from now onwards without my specific permission to do so. The press will go mad once news of the Erskine killing leaks out, and it will, judging by past experience. No one is to say anything to any journalist, whatever favours they have received in the past from any of the dangerous beggars. A press conference with the Chief Constable has been fixed for first thing tomorrow morning. In the meanwhile, I want DS Travers and Carter to attend Flora Erskine's post mortem. It's been fixed, provisionally, for five pm this afternoon. The body's already been ID'd. A full statement will be needed from Maria Russell, DC Littlewood…'

The briefing went on and on, but Alice's attention was elsewhere. In her mind she wandered through Flora Erskine's house in Dean Mews trying to catch a glimpse of the girl's character, her personality. The rooms had all been tidy, well-ordered, everything seemed to have a place and everything was in its place. Her desk had neat piles of paper on it and a number of different coloured pens were to hand; evidence of their use could be seen on some of the documents. She seemed to have been fond of sport—a tennis racket and hockey stick were in the hall—and also to be a keen cook. Her kitchen displayed a professional-looking array of gleaming knives and pans, and her bookcase was overfilled with recipe books. Alice's recreation of the young advocate's home ended when her shoulder was tapped by DC Littlewood. She was wanted in DCI Bell's office again. Her heart sank. Let her wait, she thought, she wanted to see whether Ant's fax had come through. On her desk was a sheaf of fax paper with a covering note on Faculty of Advocates' headed notepaper.

'Hi sweetheart, sorry not to be able to speak to you on the phone. I was in court attempting, unsuccessfully, needless to say, to interdict a woman from cutting down a leylandii hedge. I fed Elizabeth Clarke, David Pearson, Flora Erskine and Tommy MacBride into the SLT database and guess what came out? The "Mair case" you mentioned, its official citation is "Mair v Lothian Health Board". I assume that this is the one you were looking for? No hits for Tommy MacBride, I'm afraid. Let me know if you need anything else. Ant.'

Alice cursed herself for not spelling out 'Sammy McBryde' to the air-headed receptionist.

As she entered the Chief Inspector's domain, Elaine Bell still had her briefing notes under one arm and was sitting on the edge of her desk examining the wallet of photographs of David Pearson. She gestured, mutely, for Alice to take a seat and continued to study the prints. The phone rang but she ignored it until, eventually, it silenced itself and she spoke.

'What do you think, Alice?'

'About what exactly, Ma'am?' she replied cautiously.

'Laura Pearson. You and Alastair have seen more of her than the rest of us put together. Could she have done it?'

'No.'

'Well, don't be coy. Explain, please'

Alice sighed. 'No, I don't think she could have done it. I don't think she even had a motive. I'd bet my life, well maybe Alistair's life, that she had no idea who Flora Erskine was, that the girl was dead or that her husband was screwing around with her. When we broke the news it shattered her, or gave every appearance of doing so. If she didn't know about Flora Erskine she'd have no reason to kill her, and I don't think she'd have touched Elizabeth Clarke either. She seems to be a very rational character, controlled, not some kind of hot-head...'.

'She's all we've got,' Elaine Bell said desperately.

'Maybe, but it's a bit thin. Even if she did have a motive, what else is there? She's small and two full-grown men were overpowered. One of them was a labourer, she couldn't have managed that. The prints in Bankes Crescent, the Medway and the Mews are not hers, whoever else's they may be. Her accomplice? Not a shred of evidence about that, if so. On the other hand she is clever, she knew where all our questions were going and she gives the impression of something, someone, forged by fire, capable of taking much more than most without buckling or breaking.'

Sensing her boss's dejection, she continued. 'One interesting thing has turned up though, Ma'am. Before I came to see you I checked my desk. I've been sent a fax by an advocate friend of mine. It's a case report involving in some way or other Dr Clarke, Pearson and Flora Erskine. It may be nothing, a mirage, but it seems worth following up. I'll get a copy to you.'

'Yes, you do that Alice,' the Inspector said wearily. 'I haven't time to read it now. Body will be coming in the next few minutes together with the Chief Constable, as somehow the press are going to have to be contained, and the conference tomorrow will be our best opportunity to prevent them from whipping up further hysteria. I'll be shut up with the pair of them dealing with the draft release for the next hour or so, but if the report's helpful in any way please let me know. We need every bit of good news that we can get at the moment. I don't envy the Chief Constable his role tomorrow at the press conference.'

'Yes, Ma'am.' Alice began to move towards the door.

'And by the way, Alice', she smiled almost sheepishly, 'I'm sorry...' She stopped herself, rephrased her thought and began again. 'I may, earlier, have been a bit sharp with you. Mrs Winter rattled the cages of the great apes who hold all our careers in their grimy palms. We could do without Wilkinson's early involvement too... but the stuff you got from Laura Pearson has been useful, very useful.'

'Yes, Ma'am.'

The report of the judgement in the Mair case was long, over twenty sides, but Alice settled herself in her chair eager to make a start. Before she had read the first few lines she was interrupted.

'Well, are you ready for action?' Inspector Manson said, standing in front of her.

'Now, Sir?' She tried to think what he might mean.

'When else? Can't let another body get cold.'

She contemplated saying nothing, following him and seeing where they ended up, gleaning along the way what they were supposed to be up to, but decided, instead, to admit her ignorance.

'I'm sorry, Sir, but I've forgotten what we're supposed to be doing.'

He looked at her pityingly. 'Alice, for Christ's sake. Time of the month or what? Didn't you listen to any of the briefing? Bell said we were to go and see Flora Erskine's parents in Cupar in case they know of any connection between McBryde and the dead woman. I'll see you at the car.' He turned and left her.

Alice closed her eyes. She could have shouted out loud in desperation, in anguish. Hours spent on a wild goose chase in the company of Inspector Manson, a face-to-face meeting with the parents of the dead girl. Their grief would be inescapable, infectious, debilitating.

And the reality proved to be worse than she had imagined. Flora Erskine was an only child, and her parents were all but speechless in their distress. Inspector Manson behaved like a clown who had inadvertently wandered into a funeral, oblivious to the mood, determined only to perform. She returned to the office after eight pm, exhausted, picked up the fax and set off for home.

13

OUTER HOUSE
(LORD CAMPBELL-SMYTH)
PROOF: JUNE 2005
JUDGEMENT: NOVEMBER 2005

MAIR v. LOTHIAN HEALTH BOARD

Counsel for the Pursuer:
Russell Silverburgh QC
Mary Garner, Advocate.

Counsel for the Defender:
David Pearson QC
Flora Erskine, Advocate.

'The pursuer in this action of damages is Teresa Bernadette Mair, mother and guardian of Donald David Mair, born on 10th January 1999. The defenders are Lothian Health Board and they are sued on the basis of their liability for the acts and omissions of Dr Elizabeth Clarke, Consultant Obstetrician and Gynaecologist and Dr Paul Ferguson, Senior House Officer, employees of the Royal Infirmary, Edinburgh.

Donald David Mair (hereinafter referred to as "Davie") was born in the Royal Infirmary at approximately 17.10 hrs on 10th January 1999. He was the pursuer's fifth child and all four of her previous children were born in the same hospital. Consequently, that institution was familiar with Ms Mair's obstetric history. Her first child, Joanne, was born by emergency Caesarean section in 1990, her second child, Kelsie, was born by normal spontaneous vaginal delivery in 1993, her third child, Shane, was born by emergency Caesarean section in 1995 and her fourth child, Alex, was born by normal spontaneous vaginal delivery in 1997. After the birth of her third child, Shane, the pursuer developed an infection in her Caesarean section wound requiring treatment by antibiotics. The wound healed after approximately one month. The pursuer's four children all took the surname of their father, John Bradley, to whom the pursuer was then married. In early 1997 the pursuer and John Bradley separated, the pursuer then reverting to her maiden name of Mair, and by 1998 the Bradleys were divorced. In July 1997 the pursuer began cohabiting with Samuel McBryde and thereafter Davie was conceived. Originally, Mr McBryde was a joint pursuer, suing on behalf of his son, but he abandoned his part in the action following the break up of his relationship with Ms Mair in 2004.

The pursuer's obstetric history, prior to Davie's birth, is of critical importance in this litigation. Professor Harold Drew, Sanderson Professor and Head of the Department of Obstetrics and Gynaecology at the University of Glasgow, was adduced as an expert witness on the pursuer's behalf. He opined that when Ms Mair attended the Royal Infirmary with her fifth pregnancy she was at a higher than normal risk of complications during delivery. In particular, in the light of her two previous Caesarean sections she was at increased risk of uterine rupture, i.e. a rupture of the womb. The fact that she had previously experienced infection in her Caesarean section scar further increased this risk. Accordingly, the Professor was in no doubt that when Ms Mair attended the Royal Infirmary, in her fifth pregnancy, she should have had discussed with her the various modes of delivery open to her and the risks and benefits associated therewith. She should have been informed that she could, prior to the onset of labour, undergo an elective Caesarean section and that this would probably be the least hazardous option for the baby. Alternatively, she could undergo a short trial of natural labour which would end either with a normal spontaneous vaginal delivery or an emergency

Caesarean section. She should also have been informed that an emergency Caesarean section in labour involves a significantly higher degree of morbidity for the mother than either spontaneous vaginal delivery or elective Caesarean section. Professor Drew explained that, with the pursuer's obstetric history, it would be particularly necessary to discuss possible modes of delivery with her because, if any complications were to arise, they might produce catastrophic consequences. Such complications would include the rupturing of the womb. If such a rupture were to occur then a hysterectomy might be required. Further, such a rupture could result in sudden and severe fetal asphyxia i.e. interference with the respiration of the baby such that its tissues neither receive enough oxygen nor can get rid of carbon dioxide. Such asphyxia could result in severe brain damage to the unborn child. Professor Drew was adamant that if such information was not transmitted to Ms Mair at the time of booking, during the pregnancy or prior to the onset of labour, then this would constitute a standard of care which would fall below that of the ordinary consultant obstetrician or senior house officer acting with ordinary care and skill. In short, such a failure would constitute medical negligence. I have no hesitation in accepting the views expressed by Professor Drew and the defenders adduced no evidence to suggest that such a duty would not be incumbent upon those caring for the pursuer throughout her fifth pregnancy.

Accordingly, one of the critical questions in the present case is was the necessary information passed on to Mrs Mair? Evidence in relation to this matter came from three sources and I will deal with each separately. Firstly, from the pursuer herself. Mrs Mair was certain that at no stage in her care by the hospital had the possibility of an elective Caesarean section for the birth of her fifth child been discussed by anyone with her. She said that if she had been offered a Caesarean section, to take place prior to the onset of labour, she would have "leapt at it" as she had not enjoyed her previous experiences of natural childbirth finding the process to be exceedingly painful and exhausting. On the other hand she had recovered from her previous Caesarean sections quite speedily and already had a scar in consequence of them. In reply to Mr Pearson's skilful cross-examination she indicated that she would have remembered if someone had raised the matter with her as even she had been apprehensive about the "bursting" of her internal scar with yet another natural delivery. Secondly, evidence on this matter came from Dr Elizabeth Clarke, Consultant Obstetrician and Gynaecologist, and one of the clinicians under attack. She testified that she had not discussed the possible modes of delivery and any associated benefits or risks to mother and child with the pursuer herself as she had deputed this task to her Senior House Officer, Dr Paul Ferguson. She indicated that she had checked with Dr Ferguson, immediately following the pursuer's second last visit to hospital and prior to delivery, that he had provided Ms Mair with the necessary information so that she could make an informed choice for the delivery of her baby. Dr Ferguson informed her that he had discussed all the options available to Ms Mair with her and had, in particular, discussed the relative risks associated with spontaneous vaginal delivery, elective and emergency Caesarean section, all in the context of her previous obstetric history. Professor Drew earlier gave evidence, in cross-examination, that a Consultant, such as Dr Clarke, would be quite entitled to depute the duty incumbent upon himself or herself as long as they checked with the subordinate that the necessary information had been imparted within a suitable timescale. That described by Dr Clarke could be so classified, on the Professor's evidence.

Thirdly, the Senior House Officer, Dr Paul Ferguson, informed the court that he could clearly recall his conversation with Ms Mair about the modes of delivery open to her. He recalled her informing him that "no way" would she elect to have a Caesarean section having suffered "agonies" with her last Caesarean section and a protracted period of discomfort as a result of the wound infection associated with it. She had opted for spontaneous vaginal delivery, "nature's way" as she, apparently, described it in the knowledge that an emergency Caesarean section could be executed if the need arose. He confirmed that he had discussed with Dr Clarke all the matters adverted to by her in her evidence on the occasion described by her. There was no dispute between the pursuer and the defenders that if the pursuer had been offered, and had accepted, the option of an elective Caesarean section then all the complications which subsequently arose for the pursuer herself and, more importantly, for her son, could have been avoided.

Having considered all the evidence germane to this issue very carefully I have, reluctantly, come to the conclusion that I must prefer that provided by Doctors Clarke and Ferguson over that provided by the pursuer. It was clear, particularly in cross-examination, that the pursuer was a very poor historian. She was quite unable to recall many pertinent events whilst under the care of the hospital prior to Davie's birth. She, wrongly, maintained that she had only met Dr Ferguson on one occasion despite the fact that the hospital records clearly recorded two such meetings. She could only explain the record of the second meeting in terms of record tampering, suggesting that the reference to the second meeting had been added after Davie's birth and once the seriousness of his condition had been appreciated. She founded, in this matter, on the anomalous place in the records for the relevant entry. Dr Ferguson denied any record falsification explaining that the entry had been entered in the wrong place through error on his part. Ms Mair's evidence was often muddled and, ultimately, I have come to conclude, unreliable. Whilst I do not consider that she intended to be misleading, in any respect, I have nonetheless reached the conclusion that her recollection was untrustworthy. In any event, her evidence in relation to any alleged record-tampering, whilst not worthless, amounted to little more than speculation, depending as it did upon an assumption about the "correct" place for the second entry. No evidence was led by her Counsel from any source, to confirm that her assumption about the "correct" place for the entry was justified. I consider it probable that Ms Mair has simply forgotten the second meeting with Dr Ferguson.

I wholeheartedly accept the evidence provided by Dr Clarke. She impressed me as a conscientious witness, meticulous in considering all the questions put to her and coherent and consistent in responding to all such questions. In particular, she provided an entirely believable account of the meeting that she had with Dr Ferguson at which she checked that Ms Mair had received the information that she was entitled to receive. Further, that meeting took place within the acceptable timescale described by Professor Drew. She is, very evidently, a first-class physician. Dr Ferguson confirmed Dr Clarke's account of the meeting, including its timescale and content.

He, also, was an impressive witness. He spoke to the occasion of his second meeting with Ms Mair when he advised her *inter alia* that she could have a Caesarean section, prior to the onset of labour, and described the risks and benefits associated with elective Caesarean section, emergency Caesarean section and spontaneous vaginal delivery. As noted earlier, the records contained an entry anent a second meeting between Dr Ferguson and Ms Mair and it recorded that she had received appropriate advice relating to the modes of delivery open to her and the risks and benefits associated therewith. In all the circumstances, I do not consider that the pursuer has proved any fault on the part of either Dr Clarke or Dr Ferguson...'

Alice read on, skipping the parts of the judgement she found incomprehensible and starting again at a description of the child's birth and the consequences of it:

'... Davie was born on 10th January 1999 at 17.10 hrs. By 16.30 hrs on that date the fetal heart had dipped abnormally low to 80 beats per minute and it remained at this dangerously low level until 16.50 hrs at which point Dr Elijah was informed. Dr Elijah attended, as soon as he was able to do so, reaching the pursuer at 17.05 hrs. He performed an immediate vacuum extraction on the pursuer and the child was finally born, as noted, at 17.10 hrs. The measures taken by Dr Elijah with regard to the management of the pursuer's postpartum (after delivery) haemorrhage were entirely appropriate. He called the Consultant on call, Dr Naylor, as a matter of urgency. Dr Naylor attended, assessed the situation and performed an exploratory operation. This revealed *inter alia* that the pursuer's womb had ruptured, through the old Caesarean section scar. Attempts to suture the rupture failed and accordingly Dr Naylor required to perform a sub-total hysterectomy, involving the surgical removal of the pursuer's womb with her ovaries being retained. It was clear from the evidence that the baby's abnormally low heart rate, prior to birth, resulted from the rupture of the scar. No rupture of the scar would have occurred if the pursuer had undergone an elective Caesarean section prior to the onset of labour. Had said scar not ruptured the baby would not have suffered asphyxia in the course of his birth and gone on to develop the catastrophic brain damage attributable to it. Equally, Mrs Mair would not have experienced the postpartum haemorrhage she endured or required to undergo the sub-total hysterectomy undertaken to stop the otherwise uncontrollable bleeding.

Due to the rupture of the scar Davie's brain was subjected to severe oxygen starvation. He is now very severely physically and mentally disabled. He has been diagnosed as suffering from cerebral palsy affecting his whole body. His limbs and his trunk are subject to uncontrollable fluctuations in tone. He cannot roll, sit, crawl or stand. He will never be able to do any of these things. He requires to be carried everywhere and, at present, this is done by his mother. As his weight increases this will become increasingly difficult for her. He has no useful function in either hand. He cannot reach out for objects or hold them if they are put in his hand. He has no recognisable speech or language and possesses no means of communicating even his most basic needs. He has no understanding of speech or gesture. He screams, for no apparent reason, occasionally during the day and usually twice per night. He has no intentional movements and has joint problems affecting both hips. Both have been operated on but, nonetheless, they appear to cause him considerable discomfort. Davie has very limited cognitive function, suffering from severe intellectual impairment. He is unlikely to exceed the level of function exhibited by a 6-month old baby in this regard. Due to his brain insult he is prone to epileptic seizures. He requires, and will always require, to be fed through a tube in his stomach. He often regurgitates, or vomits, food ingested. He is doubly incontinent and will never achieve continence. He has a very disturbed sleep pattern requiring to be comforted by the pursuer, on average, six times per night. Since his birth Davie (as he has always been known by his family) has been cared for selflessly by his mother, Ms Mair. The standard of care provided by her to her son has been exemplary and his lack of hospital admissions is in itself a testament to the excellence of the care provided by her. It would be no exaggeration to say that since his birth Ms Mair has devoted her whole life to the physical and mental needs of her disabled child. Originally, she received some assistance from the child's father, Samuel McBryde, but the extent of the care provided by him appears to have diminished over time as the severity of the child's overall disability became more apparent. Unfortunately, this meant that as Ms Mair's burden increased the support provided by the child's father decreased. Fortunately, she has had one steadfast rock of support since Davie's birth, her brother, Donald Mair. He has, to the best of his ability, done everything in his power to help his sister and nephew. He has rendered physical assistance and moral support and his own marriage may well have been a casualty of his fraternal devotion.... The total claim advanced on the pursuer's behalf, which included *inter alia* the assistance of professional carers throughout Davie's life, was for £1,500,000. Had I found in her favour I would have awarded her, for the reasons adverted to above, the sum of £1,400,000. However, the pursuer has not succeeded in proving her case and accordingly no damages are payable to her...'.

Alice breathed out deeply. At last here was something that connected all four victims, even if the precise significance of the connection was not yet clear. The advocates who had successfully defended the case for the Trust were dead, and it was their efforts which had ensured that the Trust did not require to pay Ms Mair a penny in compensation. One of the doctors blamed for the catastrophe was also dead and the child's father, who appeared to have sloughed off his responsibilities, had been killed too. She went over to her scanner and patiently fed sheet after sheet into it until she could e-mail the entire judgement to Alastair, adding a note to say that she would call at his house in about an hour's time to talk about it.

14

One foot emerged through the froth of bubbles, quickly followed by the other. Somewhere under all the foam the soap was hiding and Alice searched, lazily, in the warm water for it, tracking down the soft bar to an area close to her left thigh. On the radio some man from Northern Ireland was berating an inoffensive woman for her 'unthinking' enjoyment of a film which, he claimed, denigrated the female sex as a whole and the role of the housewife in particular. With a feeling of omnipotence Alice switched him off, preferring, instead, the regular rhythm of the drip from the leaking cold tap. After a further quarter of an hour's soaking she rose slowly out of the bath and began to dry herself, her mind preoccupied with the thought that they had entered the ring for the last round and the final bell was not too far off.

Most of the cooker hood was now a bright, post-box red and Alastair climbed down the ladder to admire his handiwork, paintbrush and paint pot in hand. Stepping a few paces backwards towards the fridge to get a better view, he thought how much better the red looked than the dull grey which covered the rest of the kitchen. The sound of the door opening alerted him to his wife's approach. Ellen came and stood beside him, looked at the wall and then at him enquiringly.

'Do you like it?' he asked, knowing in advance the likely reply.

'What do you think?' she fenced, unsmiling.

He scratched his head. 'No?'

Before Ellen had a chance to answer, Alice entered the room. She sensed immediately the discord between the married couple and the reason for it was staring her in the face. Alastair smiled weakly at her.

'Well, Alice, a great improvement wouldn't you say?' but she was too canny to be drawn into their dispute, answering non-committally that both the dove grey and the pillar-box red had their charms, equal and opposite. She knew who would win in the tussle anyway; Ellen always emerged triumphant; their marital history was a chronicle of her victories. As Alastair hammered down the lid of the paint can, Ellen calmly made a pot of tea and exited the room carrying her copy of *The Times*.

'You read the judgement?' Alice asked, as her friend cleaned the paint off his hands.

'Yes, all of it. I think we'd better go and see DCI Bell. She's still in her office. I phoned earlier and Ruth said she's taken to practically living in her room.'

'Okay, but tell me what you think first?'

'I don't know exactly what to think. The killings must be connected in some way to this case, but how exactly is still a bit of a mystery. I suppose that the mother, Davie's mother, might have had a grudge against the lawyers. They represented the hospital and won the case for it. Also she blamed Dr Clarke for the state of her son. All we know about Sammy McBryde is that he left her in the lurch, to cope on her own. Maybe she's the killer… I don't know… perhaps her brother? And what about Dr Ferguson and the judge? You'd think they'd be on her list…'

As they were talking Ellen re-entered the kitchen. She was frowning and pointing to the baby monitor on top of one of the kitchen units. She demanded, 'Is that on?'

Getting no answer from her husband, she picked it up and

examined the controls on the side. 'Yes, it's on. On bloody mute mode,' she answered herself. 'So even though Gavin's been crying his eyes out you'll have heard nothing. You put him to bed again without a nappy and he's soaking, he must have been crying for ages…'

No lights were visible through the gaps around DCI Bell's office door; the room appeared to be in total darkness, unoccupied. Tentative knocking elicited a resigned 'Come in,' and as they pushed open the door a lamp was switched on. DCI Bell was in the process of raising herself from the desk on which she had been slumped. As she did so, her substitute blanket, a jacket, slid off her and onto the floor. She had a red line running down one side of her face, a deep crease made by her makeshift pillow of a scarf. The remains of her supper—sandwiches and a yoghurt—lay in a cardboard box on her desk beside an empty bottle of cranberry juice. Three files were piled up next to her, the contents of the top one spewed all over the floor.

'I should have gone home,' she said wearily.

'Maybe. Maybe not,' Alice replied, handing over, as she spoke, a copy of the Mair Judgement and beginning to provide a hurried précis. Unable to read and listen simultaneously, Elaine Bell pushed it impatiently to one side, giving Alice her full attention, stopping her only if she went too quickly or to get clarification. At the end of the summary she told them both to sit down, and they listened as she phoned DI Manson to arrange protection for Lord Campbell-Smyth and Dr Ferguson. Having done this, she smiled broadly at her two Detective Sergeants.

'Tomorrow, the pair of you will go and see Ms Mair. Have you got an address for her yet?'

'6D Bright Park, Sighthill,' Alice replied. 'It's in the judgement.'

Sleep was not elusive, it came quickly, overpowered her within minutes of her head touching the pillow. But with it did not come peace; quite the reverse, a nightmare. She was the crucial witness in a murder trial, and the killer's conviction would depend upon the impression she conveyed to the jury. They must perceive her as trustworthy, reliable, thoroughly competent. Entering the courtroom, preceded by the Court Officer, she walked in a dignified fashion towards the witness box, sensing a chill in the room. As she was about to step up into the box she became aware that she was wearing neither skirt nor shoes, although her pants and tights were on, thank God. She glanced at the jurors, a group of irate baboons, chattering and baring their teeth at each other, apparently oblivious to her presence, and turned round and retraced her steps to the door.

Having left the court, she raced to the witness room in search of her missing clothes; and there, on a trestle table, were heaps of ladies' garments such as might be found on a chaotic second-hand stall in a market. Feverishly she tore into the first pile, unearthing discoloured underwear, knitted leggings, nylon pyjamas and, finally, a skirt. In her desperation its gingham pattern could be overlooked, but it had no zip or other fasteners, and billowed down to her ankles as soon as she let go of the waistband. Redoubling her efforts she attacked the second pile, throwing aside bibs, petticoats and slacks, until she unearthed another skirt, black and with the zip intact. Having got it on, she swivelled it round to the front, only to discover a vast white stain extending from thigh to thigh, but it would have to do. Time was of the essence, and with every second that ticked past, the trial was being held up due to her non-appearance.

Sprinting through the courtroom door she saw the Court Officer. He was frowning and gesticulating theatrically with his hands to tell her to slow down. She obeyed and padded across the floor towards him, realising as she was doing so that she still had no shoes on. Disdain at her shoeless state was written across his face, and she knew, with complete certainty, that without footwear her evidence would be valueless, so much chaff, and the accused would get off. The eyes of the Advocate-Depute questioning her did not meet her own, but returned, time after time, to her breasts, until she allowed her own eyes to glance downwards at her front. Three slices of buttered toast were peeking, incongruously, out of her bra. The voice in her head told that the answer was to eat them, so she started to crunch her way through the first one.

'All along you have maintained that the first, and best, way to extricate oneself from such an extraordinary meeting, might be to utilise the known, tried and tested methods?' the Advocate-Depute said, leaning towards her and then plunging his hands into his pockets in a highly mannered fashion.

'Wash sthat a quessstionsh..?' Alice replied, mouth full of toast, spattering crumbs as she spoke, and noticing that one had adhered to her inquisitor's upper lip.

'Today, as every day, there can be little, if any, doubt of the overall tenacity of the proposition advanced in terms of, if nothing else, its validity and inherent coherence, not to mention its internal consistency in the face of multiple challenges?'

He might as well be speaking Chinese. Alice watched, with horror, the advocate lick his lips in anticipation of her answer and then chew the stray particle he had found.

'Er... I'm not entirely sure that I have understood the question,' she said, noticing out of the corner of her eye that one of the baboons in the jury was attempting to get the judge's attention by waggling its blue hindquarters out of the jury box.

Alice's dream anxiety ended when she was woken by a sharp rapping noise and Quill's demented barking. Still drowsy with sleep, she edged her legs over the side of the bed and sat, rubbing her eyes and yawning. Another loud knock immediately restored her senses. Christ! This must be what happened to Flora Erskine, she thought. The girl opened her front door and found behind it her nemesis, knife poised to strike. A cold shiver ran down Alice's spine. If she were to survive she would need a weapon. She tiptoed into the kitchen, inadvertently releasing the excited dog, and grabbed a bottle of wine from the rack. Her heart began to race and she leant back against the work-top, breathing in and out slowly, trying to calm herself and control the panic that she could feel rising within her.

Advancing into the corridor she was surprised to see Quill, tail wagging from side to side, whining piteously and scratching a corner of the front door. He appeared to know the killer. With her right hand raised behind her head, she yanked open the door, readying herself to smash the stranger's skull as he launched his attack. But standing on the doormat was the tiny, chittering figure of Miss Spinnell, blinking rapidly, completely oblivious to her near-death experience.

Exhaling loudly, and silently cursing the ancient pensioner, Alice deposited her weapon on the stone tenement floor and escorted the old lady into her kitchen. No doubt there would be some explanation for the unexpected night visit, even if none seemed to be anticipated from her by her visitor, despite her makeshift club. Miss Spinell fixed her neighbour with her bloodshot eyes, each orb disconcertingly having an independent life of its own.

'They've come back,' she whispered dramatically.

'Who?' Alice whispered in response.

'The thieves. They've gone too far this time. They crept into my room, while I was sleeping, and took my spectacles. Removed them from my bedside table. God knows they may have taken more, but I can't see to tell. It's a miracle they didn't hurt me as I slept. They may still be in the flat... for all I know.'

'Would you like me to go and see?'

'For heavens sake! I'm telling you that there are intruders in my home… There could be more than one of them. Phone the police,' the old woman demanded angrily.

'Miss Spinnell, I am the police, remember…'

'You're just a chit of a girl. There may be men. Big men. We need a constable, at least.'

'Don't worry, I'll just do a quick preliminary check and I'll take Quill with me. He'll be sure to warn me if any of them are left.'

'No!' Miss Spinell shrieked, 'Don't take Quill. He might get hurt!'

So Alice set off on her own, unprotected but unconcerned, and her neighbour sat with Quill at her side, sipping the only restorative that she would accept, cherry brandy. The furniture in Miss Spinell's bedroom consisted of a narrow, single bed and a bedside table. On the floor, by the table, lay the missing glasses as if they had been knocked off in the search for them, a scrabbling hand sending them flying spacewards. Alice picked them up and inspected them. They were unbroken, frame and lenses intact. The rest of the flat bore no signs of any intruders, but Miss Spinell remained unconvinced, despite Alice's account of her search.

'The men must have dropped them,' the old lady explained patiently.

'Well, I don't know,' Alice said gingerly, 'maybe they were never there. After all, why of all the items in your flat would they home in on your spectacles?'

'What better way to disable me than to rob me of my spectacles?' the old lady said impatiently. Alice said nothing. It would only scare the poor woman more if she was to point out the obvious, that age and infirmity had disabled her long ago, blind or sighted, and that a child of six would be capable of putting up more effective resistance. For a few seconds she debated with herself—should she explain to Miss Spinell that she had never, at any stage, been in peril from any intruders, or should she go along with the old lady's version of events, allow her the satisfaction of being right at the price of letting her remain prey to the thought that strange men could enter her stronghold at will? She opted for the latter; familiarity with her neighbour had taught her that nothing upset the old lady more than evidence of her own confusion. She would be comforted by the false vindication, however odd its logical consequences might be.

'I'm sure you're right, Miss Spinell. Now would you like to take Quill down to spend the rest of the night with you?' Alice offered.

The strange eyes twinkled with joy, a broad smile transformed the sunken mouth, and a look of pure pleasure swept across the aged face.

'Oh thank you, dear. It possibly would make sense.'

They walked downstairs together, Quill trotting ahead, and Alice waited until all the locks had been rammed home before returning to her bed. Four-forty-five am, and she would have to be up by seven at the latest if the dog was to get even a half decent walk. Back under the covers, she flicked anxiously through the judgement again as if simply touching the paper might, in some inexplicable way, provide more enlightenment. Her eyes fell, at random, on the word 'unreliable', and she continued reading the paragraph, unearthing 'misleading', 'untrustworthy' and 'worthless' as she did so. She would have to remember to tell the Boss tomorrow. Desperate for sleep, she forced herself to think of Druimindarroch, a real place and as close to heaven as she could imagine, a bay where the sea is always still, its unrippled surface more like glass than water. A late summer evening, the sun still in the sky, windless, and she would take the boat out beyond the island. But she never reached it, sleep always coming before she passed the old stone and slate boathouse guarding the entrance to the bay.

15

Friday 16th December

Who is responsible for the naming of the new streets, new parks and new estates in a city? Whoever it was in Edinburgh slipped up with 'Bright Park', a misnomer so crass as to hint at a sense of humour, albeit one blacker than jet. The expectations that might naturally arise from such a label could include light, airiness, space and, possibly, green leaves, but not eight concrete tower blocks plonked down in a sea of pitted tarmac, a million shards of smashed glass in each pothole, and the unsightly whole encircled by a busy ring road. Two shops, timorous behind shutters and barbed wire, served the residents, and 'community' sculptures littered the estate as if 'art' might obliterate its ugliness rather than highlight it.

The lift was broken, so the Detective Sergeants had to trudge up the endless stairs to the sixth floor, inhaling the reek of stale ammonia with every step. Flat D lay directly ahead, and sellotaped to its cream-painted front door was a hand-made notice saying 'Mair'. As Alice knocked it swung open, revealing a windowless hall stripped of furnishings and floor coverings. The place was deserted; the only furniture in it was a three-legged wooden table with an old fishtank perched precariously on top of it. The glass walls of the tank were coated in a greenish scum and a mass of dry, black weed was stuck to its base. On the bottom, with desiccated fronds collapsed over it, was a miniature pink fairytale castle, once the home of angelfish. The sounds of hoovering and Radio 2 could be heard through the door of 6E, and the plastic nameplate spelled out 'A. Girvan'. An elderly woman carrying a baby answered the door and glanced at their identity cards, pursed her lips and whispered 'The polis'.

'Sorry to bother you,' Alice explained. 'We were hoping to see Teresa Mair, but she seems to have moved. Do you have an address for her?'

'Teresa's got nae address, she's deid. You'se are too late to see her,' the woman replied, cradling the child in one elbow and wiping its mouth on its bib with her free hand.

'When did she die? Can you tell us what happened?' Alastair asked, impatient for information.

'Aye, come oan in.'

Once she had started to speak the woman seemed unwilling to stop.

'Teresa took her ain life. She done it late November. Took an overdose, in the flat wi' her ain tablets. The kids were split up soon aifter, poor wee things deserved better than that aifter a' they'd been through. They'd had...'

Alice interrupted the flow. 'Have you any idea why she killed herself?'

The rejoinder was immediate. 'Oh aye, I'd bet ma pension oan it. She'd had enough, couldnae take ony mair, naebody much could hae.' She deposited the now sleeping baby on the corner of the settee on which she was seated, and, lighting up, carefully turned her head to blow the first puff of smoke away from the child.

'You ken aboot Davie, her wee boy?' the woman asked.

'Yes. We know about him and the court case about him,' Alice responded.

'I reckon that the court case wis the final straw, fer her. See, she'd pinned a' her hopes oan it, fer the faimily like, an' once she'd heard they'd lost she couldnae cairry oan. Mind, the wee yin wis her life. The other kids never got a look-in, there wisnae time and onyway she wis worn oot. She telt me that the court money would solve a' their problems, they'd get a wee hoose somewhere nice, the special equipment that Davie needed an' mebbe even someyin to help noo an' then. Then Kelsie and the rest of them could be normal kids again an' she'd hae plenty o' time for them a'. She even talked aboot taking them on a holiday somewhere, mebbe Arran. Of course, aifter Sammy left...'

'Sammy, Samuel McBryde?' Alice enquired.

'Aye, Sammy McBryde, the wee laddie's dad. You ken', the yin that wis killed, it's been in a' the papers. Him. Onyway, aifter he left Teresa she wis devastated, she just lived on her nerves. I never seen him do much for the boy, but I suppose he wis in the hoose at least an' he did help a bit wi' the other kids, as much of a daddy to them as John Bradley ever wis. Teresa wis suicidal aifter he walked oot, but she kept hangin' oan, she reckoned that once they got their compensation a'thing would be alright again. Telt me that they lawyers had assured her that she had a guid case, that if it went to court she'd win, but more likely a big offer'd be made to keep it oot o' the courts. Donny said...'

'Donny?'

'Her brother, Donny, Donald Mair. He's her only brother, only faimily, in fact. Donny said she should take a break, he'd look aifter the kids fer her an' she could hae a few days to hersel'. He'd aye helped her oot, but aifter Sammy scarpered he wis never awa' from her hoose. I'm no' surprised Marie threw Donny oot, I'd hae daen the same, he wis never there. Nothing wis too much trouble fer him where Teresa, Davie an' the kids were concerned.'

'Who found Teresa?'

'He did. Donny. Came in here tae phone the polis an' he wis as white as a sheet, he'd been sick, ken. Kept saying o'er an' o'er that she shouldnae hae daen it. He wis shaky, like. I got him some tea an' the kids spent that night here wi' me.'

'Where are the kids?' Alice asked.

'The Bradley yins, Joanne, Kelsie, Shane and Lexie an' a' went tae their dad in Glasgow. He used tae visit regular-like an' sometimes they'd stay wi' him in Whiteinch. Davie's gone tae foster parents in Musselburgh. I spoke tae the social worker who picked him up an' she said they'd be trying to find a permanent hame fer him, but she wisnae too hopeful, said disabled children were difficult tae place.'

'Was the child's father, Sammy, not considered?'

'I dae ken. Donny telt me that Sammy had been asked tae take the boy but had refused. It wouldnae surprise me, aifter he left he never came back tae see the kiddie, his own kiddie, even the yince. Donny said he'd shacked up wi' a new wuman somewhere in Granton. He'd have been useless onyway, he never lifted a finger fer Davie even when he wis aboot, an'…'

Alice interrupted, 'What about Donny then, why didn't he take Davie?'

'Oh, he tried,' Mrs Girvan replied, 'he daen everything he could tae get the Social Work to let him care for a' the kids, including Davie, but they wis having none o' it. He wanted tae keep them all togither like, but he hadnae a hope, didnae even hae a hame o' his ain, as Marie had thrown him oot by then. I think he wis sleeping oan a friend's floor most o' the time. Onyway, he blew it. I heard him bawlin' at they social workers, crying them a' the names on God's earth, even wi' the kiddies aboot. They should hae let him hae Davie though, 'cause he really did want tae look aifter him an' he kenned mair than onyone jist whit wis involved. He'd hae done onything fer the boy. It didnae seem tae matter tae him that Davie couldnae understand or dae onything, he jist adored him jist the way he wis, an' Davie seemed tae ken it. He wis such a lovely looking wee thing tae. I've got a photy, would you'se like tae see it?'

She produced a colour photo showing a smiling woman holding aloft a laughing child. Teresa Mair may have carried the weight of the world on her shoulders, but in the picture a carefree mother was showing off her beloved boy. And what a boy. Endowed with heavenly looks, eyes as blue as borage, beneath a mass of wavy, golden hair. Alice was taken aback, appalled at herself as she realised that since reading the judgement she had imagined some drooling, malformed little thing, the antithesis of the comely image now before her eyes. In a single, shameful instant the child's tragedy had become more real, and with it that of his mother.

'Do you have an address for Donny?' she asked, handing the print back.

'Aye. I've got a note of Marie's address. I dae ken if he's gone back tae her, mind. He gave it tae me as it wis the only permanent yin he had and I'd asked him fer it. I wanted to ken hoo Davie wis getting oan and a'. I used tae sit wi' him, you ken, sometimes if Teresa had tae go oot. Daen it ever since he wis a babby. All they kids cried me Granny Annie. Joanne an' Kelsie used to play wi' my older grandkids aifter they came back fae the school. Joanne loved wee Amy, my youngest yin,' the woman looked fondly at the child at her side, 'liked to be ma wee helper...'

Stenhouse Lane was a few minutes' drive, but half a world away. No.14 had been painted a sweet, ice-cream pink, and the new Georgian-style fanlight above the door was flanked by a couple of shining carriage lamps. The rest of the houses in the lane had also been prettified by their owners, and the small enclave stood as a rebuke to the council houses surrounding them with their grey harl and uniformly drab appearance.

Marie Mair was killing time. At 11.30 am she intended to catch the bus to 'The Upper Cut' in Gorgie High Street and have her black roots bleached and a trim. In the meanwhile, the minutes were ticking away nicely with the help of day-time TV, her constant companion. What sort of man would sleep with his sister-in-law if she looked like that, she wondered, concluding, on seeing Melvin, the sort that no one else much would deign to have sex with. The crisps were stale, so she put them back in the packet and took a sip of her coffee, listening intently as Melvin was harangued by the show's outspoken hostess, and then informed by his angry wife, now hugging her grossly-obese sister, that she was going to divorce him. Serves the bastard right, she thought, two-timing slimeball, and the studio, at one with her, booed loudly as Melvin exited right. The high Westminster chimes of her front doorbell interrupted another woman's confession of her lesbian longing for her boss, and Marie Mair switched the TV off to go and answer her door. It would be the news soon anyway, and she did not want the woes of the world gaining entry into her cosy nest.

She displayed little concern when shown the police identity cards, leading her two visitors into her sitting room as if such guests routinely appeared. Even when they began asking questions about her husband, no anxiety was apparent, and her tone conveyed no sense of involvement. They might have been enquiring about the milkman or the postman. Occasionally, she would interrupt to tell them how much she enjoyed *The Bill* or to confess that before she decided on dog grooming she had considered a job in the force, like that *Prime Suspect* woman.

'So, Donny moved out in about July of this year?' Alice ploughed on.

'Yes.'

'Where did he go?'

'Like I said, I'm sorry but I've no idea.'

'Mrs Girvan thought, perhaps, he'd gone to stay with a friend.'

'You mean Billy?'

'Maybe. Can you give us Billy's address?'

'He stays in Tranent. 14 Kirk Wynd.'

'Why did your husband move out?'

'I think I'll not answer that one, if you don't mind.' She smiled politely, as if they were holding a social conversation and she had signalled that this topic was, regrettably, out of bounds.

'I'm afraid I do mind,' Alice said 'We need to know. So could you tell us why your husband moved out?'

'Do I have to tell you?'

Alice nodded, amazed that the woman did not appear to have realised that she was involved in a murder investigation, rather than simply engaged in a friendly chat.

'Cause he was more interested in his sister, Teresa, and Davie and the rest of them than me. He might as well have been her husband. After Sammy left it got worse, he spent more time up at her house than in ours. I couldn't get him as much as to change a light bulb here, but he was shopping, cleaning and babysitting all hours up at Bright Park. In the end I threw him out. I'd found someone else, someone interested in me for a change.'

'You said you and Donny were living together when Davie's court case was on?'

'In June. Aye,' she nodded.

'Did he talk much about it?'

'He never stopped talking about it,' she said tartly. 'He was up at the court in the High Street every day, every single day it was on, and in the evenings he'd rave about it to me. I didn't want to know. I had my own life.'

'Did he ever mention a Dr Clarke?'

'Who's she?'

'Dr Elizabeth Clarke. She was one of Teresa's doctors for the birth. You might have seen in the papers....'

'I don't read the newspapers. But there was doctor he was mad at. Said the judge had the hots for her, maybe that was the lady doctor. Imagine that, eh, a judge and all.'

'And David Pearson, QC, did he mention him?'

'He mentioned a QC, alright. He was forever going on about him, up his own arse he said. Tore Teresa and her witnesses to shreds in the witness box.'

'Did he mention Flora Erskine ?'

'Who?'

'Flora Erskine. She was in the case too, with the QC.'

'I don't remember him mentioning that name, but he did talk about Pearson's helpers. He said he reckoned Pearson was showing off in the court half the time to impress all the other lawyers, like.'

'Have you seen your husband since Teresa died?'

'Just the once. He came to collect the rest of his clothes, and anything else he'd left behind. It was after Davie got taken away to Musselburgh.'

'How did he seem?'

'What you mean?'

'What impression did you form of his state of mind?'

'He seemed fine. He was a bit concerned having nowhere to stay, and that, and when I said that he couldn't take the photo album he lost his rag. Otherwise, he took the break-up well. I don't think he was that bothered about us splitting up or nothing, then I'd hardly seen anything of him or him, me. I've got someone else, maybe he has too, poor bitch. Why are you all interested in him anyway?'

Without answering, Alastair picked up a framed photograph which had been lying face down on a coffee table and passed it to Alice. It showed Marie Mair in flowing white wedding gown standing, hand-in-hand, with a tall, dark-haired man dressed in a grey suit.

'Donny?' Alice enquired.

'Him and me on our wedding day in 1990.'

'Have you got anything more recent?'

'Nope. Donny hated having his photo taken, he was always so self-conscious.'

The squad meeting fixed for noon was ill-attended, the room barely half full, but this time no bodies were slumped dejectedly in their seats or gazing gloomily out of the windows. The news of a hard suspect had travelled fast and reinvigorated everyone, and the absence of so many of the regulars was attributable to the speed of DCI Bell's reactions and her conviction that, finally, they might be on the right road. Copies of the photograph of Donald Mair were being circulated and Alice took the opportunity, while waiting for her boss to appear, to inspect the man, to memorise the face of their quarry. The print showed a young man with very short, dark hair, his bride's hand clasped tightly in his own. Her figure had been cropped, leaving only her hand in his and a small white triangle of her dress. The bridegroom's gaze was fixed on the ground, oblivious to any loving looks being bestowed upon him by his now invisible wife, seemingly entranced by the shine on his own black shoes. The camera had caught a shy creature, one keen to escape scrutiny, eager to return to the shadows. No wonder his wife had only been able to produce one image of him, a wedding photo, no doubt obtained under some form of sentimental duress. Alice looked up and saw Elaine Bell moving towards the board; glancing again she took in the newly made-up appearance and the spring in her boss's step.

'You all know,' she began, her voice loud, confident and cold-free, 'that we now have a good suspect. His name is Donald Mair. He is aged forty. Photographs of him, aged twenty-four, have been distributed and we are presently working on the computer to see what noticeable changes, if any, the additional years may have made. On the only occasion on which he was seen by an eyewitness he was wearing jeans and a jacket, a dark jacket, and carrying a poly bag. He comes from Edinburgh and knows the city and East Lothian well. The last known address for him was 14 Kirk Wynd, Tranent. We think that he may be responsible for the deaths of Dr Clarke and David Pearson. He seems to think that they screwed up the life of his sister, Teresa, resulting in her eventual suicide. He may have had a grudge against McBryde and Flora Erskine, too. He probably has other targets in his sights. In particular, another doctor, Paul Ferguson, and a Court of Session judge, Matthew Campbell-Smythe. Lord Campbell-Smythe to you lot, to us.

Eric Manson has already made contact with Dr Ferguson and we've got a watch over his home in Veitch Park, Haddington, and his workplace at Roodlands Hospital. Campbell-Smythe's a big fish. His home, in Drummond Place, is being watched and he's got protection at the Court of Session, beyond the norm. Half of the Forensics team are combing Mair's house in Stenhouse Lane at the moment, and the other half are on their way to his last known address in Tranent, a local authority flat tenanted by a Billy Gannon. Uniforms picked Gannon up at his work on the industrial estate in Macmerry and they're bringing him here. They should arrive within the next ten minutes or so, and he may be able to give us some clue, as a minimum, where Mair has been living for the last few weeks.

More copies of the suspect's photo are being produced so that we can circulate them to the press when the time comes. What we know about him so far is that he has no previous convictions or form of any kind but, if it's him, he's a highly effective killer. Whilst it's not difficult to see how he could gain access to Sammy McBryde—they were effectively brothers-in-law after all—he must have managed to talk his way into Dr Clarke's house and Flora Erskine's. Certainly, there were no witnesses to any scuffles or disturbances or anything like that. He's probably strong. It's likely he was able to overpower McBryde and Pearson, albeit that he had a weapon, and the element of surprise was on his side. Also, he seems well organised. The poly bag he was seen carrying in Granton Medway likely contained his bloody clothes. Forensics have always been clear that his handiwork resulted in a virtual bloodbath—most of you have seen its effects at first hand—so he'd have needed a change of togs. The bag probably also contained his weapon of choice, most likely a knife. No trace of any weapon has been found despite exhaustive searching, and the guesstimate is that the same blade, or whatever, seems to have been involved in all the killings.

His wife's being questioned again by Sandy Murray to find out as much about Mair as we can, including his friends, acquaintances, usual haunts, etc. DSs Travers and Carter are on their way to Blyths, the butchers on Gorgie Road, to speak to any employees there. Mair worked with them up until March this year—', DCI Bell stopped her speech to answer her phone. She put it back in her pocket and caught Alice's eye.

'That's the boy in. Could you and Alastair go and speak to him now?'

Gannon wanted to light up, felt the need of a smoke, but knew he was not allowed to do so. Instead, as he spoke, he folded and re-folded the silver paper from the packet over and over again, oblivious to the irritation his incessant activity was causing. Within minutes the nature of his involvement with Donald Mair became clear, and it was minimal. Gannon was an innocent, a pond-skater never breaking the surface tension of the water to see what lay below, content with appearance, aware of no other reality. He had got to know Donald Mair through a shared passion for snooker and their friendship extended no further, but on that basis he had allowed his homeless friend to kip occasionally on his floor until his own girlfriend, Angela, had kicked up about it. He had no idea where the man was now, and if pressed to guess, thought Donny might be living, or at least sleeping, in his car. He had done it before and the vehicle was crammed with clothes, blankets and black bags full of stuff. He might park anywhere.

Dr Clarke and the other victims, including Samuel McBryde, meant nothing to the man except as names in the paper, and he had never heard of Davie or Teresa unless, maybe,

Teresa was Donny's sister? His pal often left his work to see his sister, although he had no idea why.

Alice became aware, as Billy Gannon answered their questions, that despite their references to Dr Clarke and the others, the witness seemed to have made no connection between his friend and the killings. He had received more than enough information for most people to work out the thrust of their enquiries but had failed to do so. She looked at his face, noting how unlined it was. Perhaps little penetrated his skull sufficiently to cause him any anxiety, perhaps he led a charmed life. He certainly appeared to have supped regularly with the devil, emerging unscathed from their encounters.

Billy Gannon left the interview room no wiser than he had entered it. When his supervisor, at his new place of work, asked him about his trip to the police station he stated, blandly, that they had needed information about someone he used to work with. He had not gossiped; he had nothing to gossip about.

'You can't hide a car for very long,' Inspector Manson said, nodding to himself sagely before concluding authoritatively, 'We'll get him that way if no other.'

'I don't know,' Alastair chipped in, sipping his coffee and helping himself from the open packet of biscuits on his desk. 'He could easily discard it, live rough for a while, or maybe he's got more than one friend, more than one floor he can doss on...'

'He'd freeze to death living rough, it was minus three degrees last night. It's nearly Christmas,' Manson replied thickly, his mouth half-full of Alice's shortbread.

'Down and outs survive, year in year out, they can go to Jericho House or one of the other shelters. They make special provision at this time of year,' Alastair persisted, careless of persuading his colleague but keen to annoy. It couldn't all go the one way.

Alice slipped unnoticed into an alcove at the back of Court 8 and was surprised by the strange, soft, cinema-like appearance of the seats. The witness box was familiar to her, but she had rarely enjoyed the luxury of attending court as a spectator. DCI Bell would have a fit if she knew I was here, she thought, settling down into her chair, determined to see Lord Campbell-Smythe for herself. After all, his judgement had triggered Teresa Mair's suicide and exonerated Doctors Clarke and Ferguson. He had a central role in their drama; little would be lost by her concealed presence and much might be gained by it.

A female witness was attempting to explain to the court, in a low voice, what her employment as a box-packer required her to do. She was inarticulate and continually used hand gestures to show the movements she required to make, unable to describe them verbally. Every time she did so she was rebuked by the Judge, initially courteously but with signs of increasing impatience. Alice noticed that on two occasions Campbell-Smythe's eyes met those of the opposing Advocate, before rolling heavenwards to signal his exasperation. The demeanour of the woman's Counsel changed when he sensed the shared contempt of the Judge and his opponent, becoming flustered and reeling off another muddled question. His lack of confidence communicated itself to the witness, who stopped speaking in mid-sentence, keen to escape her predicament.

Alice studied Campbell-Smythe's face, realising, with surprise, that she recognised it. Glasgow High Court, 2001, the trial of William Head, an ordeal by fire from which she had emerged blistered and burnt. The accused's Counsel had been Campbell-Smythe, then plain Matthew Campbell-Smythe, QC. He had battered her, harangued her, made her feel so foolish that she had almost conceded that her certainty that she had seen Head at the crime scene had been misplaced. How could she have forgotten, for even an instant, those beetling brows and that projecting jaw, Neanderthal features concealing a piercing intellect. He had even made a pass at her later in the canteen, as if the court room pummelling had never taken place, and been surprised by the vehemence of her refusal. Rebuffed, he had whispered into her ear, 'It's just a job', leaving her feeling gauche and awkward, inexperienced in the real rules of some sophisticated play.

16

Saturday 17th December
The smell coming from the baker's was irresistible. Without conscious thought Alice found herself at the counter, eye-level with a miniature glass oven laden with hot pies, sausages and bridies, each item surrounded by its own individual pool of grease. At last, an old-fashioned shop immune to the current trend for wraps and lattices or brie-and-bacon baguettes, specialising instead in egg rolls, crisps and Irn Bru. Back at her desk she bit into the Scotch pie, savouring its cardboard pastry and peppery interior. Scanning her list as she ate, she noted with dread that she still had four more refuges left to call in the city, excluding the Salvation Army and Jericho House. Her phone rang. It was DCI Bell. 'Any results with the hostels, Alice?'

'No, Ma'am, but I've still a number to do. What about the vehicle, has it been found?'

'Not yet. Every second uniform is out looking for it, but it seems to have vanished into the ether.'

'By the way, Ma'am, in the judgement, the words "unreliable", "worthless"…' She left her sentence unfinished, on hearing the dialling tone.

The supervisor of the Pilton Shelter appeared to be in no hurry to answer. As Alice hung on and on, impatient for a reply, her mind drifted back to Mair himself. What sort of man was he? What precisely did she know about him? His wife had been cool, detatched, living in a bubble of her own creation and unconcerned about the world outside her own door. Little appeared to penetrate the mind of his friend, Gannon, but maybe Mair used him precisely because of his lack of acuity, his lack of curiosity. Then again, perhaps Mair also did not see things too clearly or chose to insulate himself from reality until life no longer let him do so. The unusual thing about their man was the strength of his attachment to his sister and nephew, a love so powerful that he had been prepared to sacrifice his own marriage in order to go on looking after them. He was impulsive, hot-tempered even; Mrs Girvan had said that he had blown any chances he might have had of caring for Davie by swearing at the social worker in Bright Park. If it was me, if I was Mair, she thought, where would I go? What would I do? The job he had set himself was unfinished, four down and two to go, he must be aware that his luck could not go on forever. It was a simple calculation; at best, a lifetime in prison, at worst he'd be killed by the police whilst attempting to complete his self-appointed task. The Bradley children were now all dispersed, and his beloved sister, dead. Only Davie remained nearby and he would know where the boy was, he could still see Davie. That's what I would do, she mused, get my fill, while I was still able to do so, of those I loved.

Without waiting any longer for the supervisor's response she replaced the receiver, dialled the City Social Work Department and was able, without the fight she had anticipated, to extract the name, address and telephone number of the child's foster parents. As she was holding on, waiting for another answer, Alastair returned to the office. He ripped open a packet of sandwiches. 'Shitey press,' he said loudly, ignoring her gesture for him to be quiet, 'they're all over the place. I had to fight my way back into the station and I got poked in the eye by one of their sodding sound booms. Of course, not as much as an apology from the swine responsible.'

Alice put down the receiver, acknowledging defeat. No reply.

'Did the skateboarder identify Mair from the photograph?' she asked.

'So so... He thinks it could have been the man he saw at McBryde's place. Who were you trying to speak to?'

'Davie's foster parents. Fancy a trip there? I've been thinking about Mair's likely whereabouts and I reckon he'll base himself somewhere close to them.'

'Why on earth should he?'

'Because before he's caught he'll want to see as much of the boy as he can. If I'm right, the Hendersons, Davie's foster parents, may already have seen Mair. It has to be worth checking out. If they have, then it's odds-on he'll return and we could have the place watched. What do you think?'

'What's the alternative?'

'Phoning round the rest of the shelters and ensuring that they get copies of the photos.'

'Why do you think he'll want to be close to the boy?'

'Because he loves him. He even wanted to look after the child himself. How many uncles do you know like that? He doesn't even have a wife in tow to help. Mair will want to be sure that the boy's in good hands as a minimum.'

'The boss won't approve. You're taking things into your own hands again, Alice. Shouldn't we check with her first?'

'No. She might say no. I'm going anyway. Are you coming or not?'

'Well, anything is better than more phone calls. Let's leave by the back entrance, avoid the swine.'

Eskside West is a pleasant, cobbled street, leading up to the old bridge and separated only by an area of municipal parkland from the broad, slow-flowing river Esk. The Hendersons' house, distinctive with its soot-blackened exterior and disabled ramp, was in the middle of an unostentatious Victorian terrace and easy to locate. No one was home. A neighbour, hauling black bags of rubbish to a skip, told them that he had seen the family leave to go shopping about an hour earlier. From the warm interior of the car, Alice gazed idly at the river. Frozen reeds protruded from its banks and the edges of the water had iced over. Seagulls paraded up and down on the grass, and two of the three arches of the bridge were blocked by mounds of branches, straw and an old tree trunk, the remnants of the last spate. In the shallows a mattress lay stranded on a bed of gravel, springs spilling out along with the rest of its entrails.

The indignant wail of a car horn drew her attention towards the traffic lights, and she noticed a family of four making their way towards the car. A man pushing a boy in a wheelchair, on his right a woman, laden with the double burden of the shopping and a baby in a sling. Their progress was slow and Alice stared at them as the boy's erratic, uncoordinated movements and bright hair proclaimed his identity. While the man wrestled with the catch on the little metal gate leading to their large front garden, the two sergeants approached. A passer-by, eyes fixed on the boy's lustrous head, bumped into Alice and mumbled an apology. She looked round, catching the stranger's eyes.

'It's him,' she said mechanically, staring at the man as he moved on.

'Who?' Alastair asked.

'Mair! Who do you bloody think!'

Her lungs were hurting, her head down, arms swinging wildly, mouth full of warm saliva. A gallon of acid must have been pumped into her chest, the pain was so intense. All her attention was on her prey, her eyes streaming and puffs of frozen breath billowing from her as she ran. Catch him, catch him, CATCH HIM. And then she fell, hard, onto the unyielding ground, legs entangled in some kind of snake-like obstruction.

Panting loudly, she raised herself up and found a toddler, reins fluttering in the wind, crying angrily beside her.

'You'll need to watch where you're going, Lucy, you've tripped the nice lady up,' the woman said, glancing apologetically at her child's victim while lifting the uninjured tot off the road. Alice ran on in the direction she had seen Mair take, increasingly conscious of an agonising pain stabbing her knee with every footfall. On the High Street she stopped to recover her breath. Gasping noisily, she stood, hands on her hips, trying to scan the pavements on either side of the busy road. A few hundred yards ahead, on the river side, she noticed a cluster of pedestrians being jostled as a dark-haired man pushed through them into an Oxfam shop. Fat bloody chance it's him, she thought, and unable to run any further, she hobbled towards her destination.

Circular racks of trousers, jackets and skirts barred her way as she crossed the shop-floor towards a counter where two elderly women, apparently oblivious to her presence, were chattering with each other. Edging past a skyscraper of stacked jigsaw puzzles, she noticed a narrow archway above which was written 'Children's Books', leading to an additional room, and limped in its direction. The man within had his back to the entrance but he wheeled round instantly on hearing the sounds of an approach.

As Alice looked in Donald Mair's eyes, she knew from the expression of fear that flitted across his face that he had recognised her as his pursuer. In that instant he launched himself at her, a human battering-ram, smashing her shoulder and the side of her face with his own. Her instinctive attempt to grab him failed, her grip broken at the sickening sensation as he slammed his knuckles into her nose. Excruciating pain engulfed her whole face and blood poured from both nostrils, streaming over her lips and cascading off her chin.

Turning round she saw Alistair blocking the doorway into the street. When Mair charged at him she watched as her friend swung a heavy wooden lamp at the man's temple, the cracking contact causing him to stop in his tracks, legs buckling beneath him as if they could no longer bear his weight.

The Hendersons were an organised pair, the sort that not only have a family first-aid box but also know where to find it and how to use it. Alice's bloodied nose was bathed and anointed by Elizabeth Henderson, while her husband busied himself making a pot of tea. They both recognised the man in the photo. He was the one who had come to their door, only a week earlier, offering to tidy up their oversized, neglected front garden.

'Did you take him on?' Alice asked, her voice uncharacteristically nasal.

'No,' Elizabeth Henderson replied, putting the hank of lint back into its box, 'He was a bit odd. The garden is a mess, and we could do with help, but we don't have the money. I told him that. Then he said he could do DIY work in the house. To be honest, he spooked me a bit.'

'Why?'

'It's hard to say. He was polite, I never felt in danger or anything, but he was so desperate, begging almost, beseeching us. I suggested that he try in Inveresk—there are big houses in that part of the town—but he wasn't interested, which seemed a bit odd. I thought he wanted to talk, but Ken thought that was fancy on my part…'

An ear-splitting shriek pierced the air and Alice looked round, startled, to find the source of the cry, and saw Davie smiling beatifically at an illuminated lava lamp. Elizabeth Henderson got up and patted his head fondly, and he appeared, momentarily, to catch her eye before returning his attention to his toy.

'Is he alright?' Alice asked, shaken, her ears still ringing from the eerie noise. 'It sounded like he was in pain or terrified of something.'

'He can't help it, and I don't think it means anything. He does it several times a day, sometimes at night too, and we're just beginning to get used to it...' the woman replied, handing her a cup of tea. 'I nearly jumped out of my skin the first time, so did Ken, even though we'd been warned. I thought the boy had been burnt or scalded, hurt in some way, but there he was, smiling sweetly away to himself.'

The kitchen door bumped open and Alastair Watt entered, Donald Mair, now in cuffs, beside him. Both men were breathing noisily and their faces were cherry-red from the exertion of the chase. Mair's head was bowed and Alice watched as he slowly raised it, took in his surroundings, caught sight of Davie and beamed. When the child, unaware of his uncle's proximity, let out a little coo of pleasure as a big bubble of red lava erupted upwards, the man's tender smile broadened. Despite the sweat running down his forehead, the curl of damp hair clinging to his bruised brow and his laboured breath, he appeared happy, as if being with Davie, simply looking at him, was enough for complete contentment.

'Can I say goodbye to the laddie?' he asked.

Without speaking, his escort moved towards the child, allowing Mair to accompany him. The prisoner placed his cuffed hands on the boy's soft curls and twirled the fine, golden hair in his fingers before kissing the crown of his head. Davie's attention, briefly, left his toy and he gurgled happily again as if aware of a familiar, benign presence at his side.

'But he doesn't want a solicitor, Ma'am,' Alice said to DCI Elaine Bell defensively.

'He needs one, so get him one anyway. The duty solicitor, please,' her superior responded.

'He's adamant that he won't have one, Ma'am. I can't force him. He says he'll speak to us but he wants nothing to do with "the law", as he calls them. He knows his rights, and I told him it would be in his interests to have a lawyer in attendance, but he's unshakeable.'

'Just get the duty solicitor, Alice. Alright?'

So Alice sat and watched as Mair talked his way into prison, the tape recorder picking up every syllable and every pause, catching every word in order for it to be used against him. His legal representative might have been on Mars for all the attention he paid to her increasingly desperate attempts to protect him from himself. As he spoke it was like witnessing the actual moment when the dam bursts, the instant when the might of all the accumulated water causes the first crack in the massive structure and it forces its way out, splintering and smashing everything in its way.

'I did do it,' he began. 'I killed them and each of them deserved exactly what they got…' Alice nodded as if she understood, and, encouraged, Mair continued.

'Teresa's at rest now. We thought we'd get justice from the courts, but they are not courts of justice—injustice, more like. I know, I was there every day, so I saw it for myself. Teresa was not, WAS NOT, offered a Caesarean section by anyone…' His voice rose in anger and he looked round as if to ensure that he had everyone's full attention. Again, Alice nodded sympathetically at him, but she said nothing.

'I know that. That's what caused all the trouble, believe me. She was petrified, shit-scared, before Davie was born, she didn't want to go through it all again, and if she'd known she could have had a section she'd have been at the front of the queue. We'd talked all about it, long before the laddie was born. But that Dr Ferguson said in court, in the actual courtroom, that he'd offered her one and she'd turned it down. Just lies from start to finish, but, of course, it was just her word against his, and you should have seen him, smart suit, smart tie, with the plums fairly falling out of his mouth. He'd even fixed the records, the hospital's own records. There was no second meeting! When Dr Ferguson said it was supposed to have happened, Teresa, Sammy and the kids were on holiday in Ayr, but Teresa only remembered that once she got home after the trial was over and when she was talking to Granny Annie about it… so that Dr Clarke was lying when she said she'd checked with Ferguson and he'd said he'd offered…'

'Why?' Alice asked, 'Why should Dr Clarke have been lying?'

'I told you, she must have been lying, because Teresa was not offered a Caesarean section by anyone, I said…'

Alice interrupted. 'Maybe she was telling the truth. It's possible that she did ask Dr Ferguson and he, to protect himself, lied to her. She was his boss after all. He wouldn't want to admit to her that he'd failed in something so important.'

'Naw,' he shook his head, 'they're all liars. They're all in it together. Protecting each other, like, protecting the hospital too. And the judge was no better. He believed every word she said. She could have been singing nursery rhymes to him and he would have been happy enough. He couldn't take his eyes off her, bewitched by her he was, and, make no mistake, she knew it. Smiling at him in her expensive suit and expensive shoes… and poor Teresa could hardly find the money for a new skirt for her own court case. You see, everything went on the kids, and she needed, she really needed that compensation money...'

'Why did you kill Sammy?' Alastair asked.

'Because he deserved it!' Mair responded immediately and aggressively.

'Why did he deserve it? We need to know. Tell us, please,' Alice said, keen to placate him and keep the flow running.

'Because the wee shite left her to drown when she depended on him. She bloody loved him, too. Sammy was fine when the wean was a baby. Claimed him then, acted the proud dad even, but once things got hard, once the doctors started to say that he wasn't right, that he would never be right, then Sammy didn't want to know. Never changed him once, never got up in the night once. When Davie's screaming began he'd just leave the house… leave it all… leave it all to Teresa. He was a useless cunt but he broke her heart when he left… and he wouldn't even help her with the court case. She might never have killed herself if he'd stayed. It wasn't because he'd found out anything… He didn't know. I checked on that before I killed him.'

'Found out? Found out what?' Alice asked, puzzled.

'That he wasn't the dad.'

'Do you know who the dad was?'

'Of course I know. I was, I am.'

Noting the sergeants exchanging glances, Mair bellowed at them, 'I know what you're bloody thinking, but you're wrong! It wasn't incest and that's not why he's the way he is, it was the birth! I was adopted by Teresa's parents when I was 10. Okay? You must be sick, the pair of you. I took their name, Mair. We are not blood relations, I've got no fucking blood relations. I don't know how it happened with Teresa, it shouldn't have, but it did, and just the once, believe it or not. But it was not incest. Davie should have been perfect. You've seen him, he would have been, if it wasn't for those fucking doctors. Teresa and I knew from the moment he was born that he was mine. There's photos of me as a baby and he was the split. Got the same birthmark even.'

'How are you so sure that Sammy never knew?'

'I told you. I made certain. When I saw him, before, like, we had a wee chat, I brought some cans and he was happy to share. I asked him if he fancied having a kid with Shona and he said no, one was enough for him. I said how come he never saw Davie? He said he didn't care, and never wanted children anyway, didn't like them. Sammy. He was just a fucking animal. I'd have looked after Davie even if he wasn't mine. I'd have done it for the wee boy himself and for Teresa…'

'Why the lawyers? Why were they to blame in all of this? What had David Pearson ever done to you?' Alastair interrupted.

'You know perfectly well.'

'No. No, I don't.'

'He and his sidekick got the hospital off, didn't they? The Infirmary would have had to pay up if it hadn't been for them. The doctors destroy Teresa and Davie's lives and walk away scot-free, all thanks to the top QC, Mr Pearson. You should have seen him in action. He fairly laid into Teresa, all oh-so-politely. He got her so confused she wouldn't have been able to give you the day of the week. Made it sound as if she was lying when she was the only one in the whole fucking building who was telling the truth. "So, Ms Mair," he says, all hoity-toity, "on a previous occasion you did turn down a Caesarean section?" and she said she had, she never said she hadn't. But this pregnancy was different, she was so scared. Then he goes on, "But you expect us to believe that this time if you had been offered the same procedure you would have given a completely different answer and gone for the section?" and she said she would have. Because she would have. And all the time he keeps glancing at that Erskine woman, and she smiles back at him, like they'd scored a point in a match or something. I overheard them, the pair of them, talking together, and they were laughing away and do you know why? A video of Davie's day had just been played in the court, showing his routine if you like, and there he was smiling, like he's always smiling, only this time at the camera. "His lovely looks will add a couple of noughts to the figure for damages," the QC says wittily, and his girlfriend laughs. That's the way they look at things.

The judge wasn't much better. He got so impatient with Teresa when she was muddled that she panicked. She could hardly speak, she was so nervous, and then when Pearson started to get things all mixed up for her she was nearly in tears. You'd think she was fucking on trial or something. The judge didn't help her, he just kept saying "Keep your voice up, please, Ms Mair", as if she could help herself, and "Please answer the questions you've been asked", when she couldn't understand the fucking question, never mind answer it. I seen him, too, the judge, I mean. I was sitting outside the courtroom at the end of the last day, and there he was, as bold as brass, talking and laughing with Pearson, like they were all dressed up for some kind of game, but now they could relax as the contest was over and the spectators had gone home. A fake wrestling bout or something.

And every day Teresa goes home to Davie and the other kids in that flat and she believes, she still believes, that because she's told the truth they will get the compensation and they'll be able to buy a proper house. Like the one she seen in all the experts' reports, wi' a garden for Davie, and a ramp, and special equipment too. She believes it! Her baby... our baby... was damaged, through no fault of hers, and all she's asking for is the means to make his life and the other kids' lives, better. And if there was any fucking justice that's what would have happened. But what she didn't know, what we didn't know, was that they were all in it together, Dr Clarke, Dr Ferguson, Pearson, Flora Erskine and the judge. All old pals together, on the same side, playing their game to their rules, and Teresa didn't understand any of it. She believed she'd get the money because she'd told the truth... and she'd made such plans, told the kiddies they'd have a room each, have holidays like other families, get a car... maybe even get some help wi' Davie. She was so bloody trusting. Then she fucking goes and kills herself...' Mair broke down in tears and Alice, instinctively, put her arm around his shoulders.

This should not happen, she thought, the boundaries should remain clear, delineated in black and white, not dissolving into shades of grey. This man had taken the lives of four innocent people. Smashed his fist into her face. But the distorted picture of the courtroom drama he had conjured up had been instantly recognisable to her. She, too, had been bamboozled by procedures and formalities, had strained to make sense of that arcane world and prevent its denizens from manipulating her within it. Gruff judicial admonishment had robbed her of the power of thought and of the ability to speak, and an oblique approach in cross-examination had left her unsure of the significance of her own answers, afraid to volunteer anything in case it could be used against her. The camaraderie she had witnessed between opposing Counsel had troubled her, seemed sinister, although it had been explained that they were all hired guns who would as easily, and as willingly, argue the opposite case, having no conviction, however passionate they might seem in court. Alice was familiar with the cosy establishment club in which professionals respect each other and honour their arcane rituals, but view with suspicion those outside it; those like Teresa Mair with no letters after their names and an unashamed fondness for daytime television.

'What happened on the day Teresa died?' Alice asked gently.

'She sent all the kids except Davie off for the day's school. She kept him back 'cause he gets home early from his special school. She asked her neighbour, Granny Annie, Annie Girvan, to watch him, saying that he'd a wee cold so she'd kept him off, and asking if it'd be okay for her to go up town to do a day's shopping. Then she went back to the flat and took all the sleeping tablets she'd got. I think she knew I'd find her, 'cause I'd said I'd come to the flat about two. She needed Davie's bath-sling adjusted and she couldn't do it herself.

She left a wee note, and you know what it said? Just one word, "Sorry". Sorry, for fuck's sake! She should have been the last person in the whole world to say sorry. She had nothing to apologise for. She looked after John Bradley's kids better than anyone else could have done and they were happy, then Davie came and nothing, *nothing* was too much trouble for her. She'd be up half the night stroking his head and then get the rest of the kids off and take him to his hospital appointments, with no car or nothing, then do all the washing, cleaning, shopping. She never stopped, and all she was asking for was what she was due. Their future depended on it. If she'd had that section Davie would have been born fine, just another kiddie like the rest of them. Granny Annie even tried to tell that David Pearson man the truth. She'd tried to say that Teresa had told her that she was scared, that she didn't want another childbirth, but she was shut up completely, and every time she tried to get it out the judge kept saying, "Could you just restrict yourself to the questions that you've been asked, Mrs Girvan".'

'And the bits of paper... you know, with the writing on them. They're from the judgement?' Alice asked.

Mair smiled, pleased to solve the riddle and take the credit.

'Yes, I wanted everyone to know. I wanted them to know that it was me killing the people involved and why they had to die. The papers connected them all, eh? You got it. I took the words from Theresa's judgement. I kept the copy she'd been given by her lawyers. That fucker wrote that my sister was "unreliable", "untrustworthy" and the like, but he got it all wrong. The QC, he was the misleading one, it was Sammy who was worthless. I'd like to have got Dr Ferguson first, because he seemed to really enjoy lying, he was the one that frightened Teresa the most. She couldn't believe he'd just make up a whole conversation with her, or that he'd alter the hospital records. She was shocked, genuinely shocked, that a professional would behave like that. It had never crossed her mind, before the case came to court, that Dr Ferguson would do that. The lawyers had told her that it would be her word against his, but she thought he'd realise he'd made a mistake, she didn't think a doctor would just lie about something so important. I don't know what word I'd have chosen for a cunt like that.'

'How did you get in to see Dr Clarke in Bankes Crescent?' Alastair asked.

'Easy. I knew where she worked and followed her home. I knocked on her door and asked to speak to her about Teresa. She remembered, of course, and I was surprised how simple it was. Guilty conscience, maybe. I don't know. Anyway, she just let me in…'

'And Sammy?'

'No problem. Sammy didn't know I hated him, I didn't always. When he lived in Bright Park we used to go out for a pint together occasionally. Like I said, I'd brought along a couple of cans… Next thing I knew I was in, and he was telling me all about his new life with Shona. It was all Shona this and Shona that and how they wanted to move out of Granton. He didn't give a shit about Teresa or Davie, cut them out of his life like they were disposable…'

'How did you get to Flora Erskine?'

'That was a bit more difficult. I had to take a chance with her. I'd followed her from the High Street a few times, so I knew where she lived, and I'd watched her, I knew she lived alone. I'd seen her in court too. I got to know all her movements. Then, on the night I rang the doorbell and she came to the door, I just pushed her in. There was no chain or nothing. One minute I was on the doorstep, the next I was in her hall with her. She was easy anyway, small and frightened. Quite different from how she seemed in court, all puffed up in her black gown and wig. I felt sorry for her, nearly changed my mind, but then I remembered her laughing at Pearson's fucking jokes about Davie's good looks and it wasn't too difficult.

Pearson, now Pearson, he was a challenge. I'd followed him, too, to his old nice house, his lovely house, up near Morningside, and I'd seen his wife and some old woman who kept popping in and out. So I knew that'd be tricky, and then there was his fucking bike too. But I got lucky. I was up at Parliament House late one evening trying to work out what to do about the judge and I saw someone come out and recognised him: David Pearson QC, no less and he started walking home.

His bike was fucked, I think. I had the knife on me, nowhere safe to leave it, in the pocket of my parka. I think God was on my side, really. It started pelting down, bucketing, so hard it was difficult to see. It was my chance and I took it. No one else seemed to be about in the Meadows, so I killed him there and then. Used a ciggy packet for the word, the only paper I had. The blood went everywhere but the rain helped a lot, and no-one would look twice in weather like that at a soaking man in an old parka. Didn't seem to be anybody about anyway, and my car, by chance, was really close. In Chambers Street, just down from the Meadows…'

'All those people killed for Teresa and Davie,' Alastair said, thinking out loud.

'No,' Mair corrected him, 'not just for them, although that would have been enough. For all the other Davies too, and their mums. It was someone's fault that Teresa killed herself, and someone's fault that Davie was born damaged, but no one would have paid. Well, now they have, and Clarke, Pearson and Erskine won't be able to bugger up anyone else's life and Sammy won't let any other woman down. I'm only sorry I couldn't finish the job, get the judge and that liar. That would have been justice, but this time played by my rules.'

Though he continued speaking for a further ten minutes, Donald Mair said nothing new but returned, time after time, to the injustice done to his sister. It was his obsession and his torment, and it had transformed an ordinary, kind man into some sort of pitiless avenging angel.

With the job done, exhaustion set in, leaving Alice on the edge of tears. The pain in her nose had returned with a vengeance, and she felt dirty and dishevelled, in need of fresh air. She collected her coat from its hook, listening, as she did so, to the sounds of hearty laughter coming from the murder suite, all tension now spent and a trip to the pub imminent. But she had no stomach for celebration.

She left the car near the Palace of Holyrood and walked slowly, with Quill at her heels, towards the ruins of St Anthony's Chapel. She followed the eastern path to Dunsappie Loch and then climbed more steeply to Salisbury Crags. By the time she reached the cleft at Cat's Nick, dusk had fallen and the cold light of the full moon had turned the rock crimson, deepening the shadows between the columns and silvering her route. Gentle rain began to fall, but she persevered, undeterred, until her feet were on the summit of Arthur's Seat, and only then, breathless, did she allow herself a rest. Her bodily aches and pains had not silenced the insistent voices in her head, demanding an answer. How could Mair have seen so much and yet so little? How could such a man have killed so many people? She had no answer.

Alice looked down onto the myriad lights of the city twinkling benignly below her, and watched as a single, flashing blue one moved slowly and inexorably in her direction.